JESSI'S WISH

I helped Danielle to work on her letter, even though she didn't seem to need much help. She wanted to talk, though. "You know what my dad says to my little brother and me each night before we go to sleep?" said Danielle. "He says, 'wish on the North Star'. That's the bright star in the sky. I never tell him, but I always make *two* wishes on the star. I wish that my family and I could go to Disney World. We've never been there. And I wish to graduate from the fifth grade and go to middle school."

When the club meeting was over, the kids ran noisily out of the room. Except for Danielle, whose mother picked her up. Danielle was tired and droopy. As they walked down the hall, I made a wish of my own. I wished that Danielle would recover.

Also in the Babysitters Club series:

Kristy's Great Idea
Claudia and the Phantom Phone Calls
The Truth About Stacey
Mary Anne Saves the Day
Dawn and the Impossible Three
Kristy's Big Day
Claudia and Mean Janine
Boy-Crazy Stacey
The Ghost at Dawn's House
Logan Likes Mary Anne!
Kristy and the Snobs
Claudia and the New Girl
Goodbye Stacey, Goodbye
Hello, Mallory
Little Miss Stoneybrook . . . and Dawn
Jessi's Secret Language
Mary Anne's Bad-Luck Mystery
Stacey's Mistake
Claudia and the Bad Joke
Kristy and the Walking Disaster
Mallory and the Trouble with Twins
Jessi Ramsey, Pet-Sitter
Dawn on the Coast
Kristy and the Mother's Day Surprise
Mary Anne and the Search for Tigger
Claudia and the Sad Goodbye
Jessi and the Superbrat
Welcome Back, Stacey!
Mallory and the Mystery Diary
Mary Anne and the Great Romance
Dawn's Wicked Stepsister
Kristy and the Secret of Susan
Claudia and the Great Search
Mary Anne and Too Many Boys
Stacey and the Mystery of Stoneybrook
Jessi's Babysitter
Dawn and the Older Boy
Kristy and the Mystery Admirer
Poor Mallory!
Claudia and the Middle School Mystery
Mary Anne vs. Logan
Jessi and the Dance School Phantom
Stacey's Emergency
Dawn and the Big Sleepover
Kristy and the Baby Parade
Mary Anne Misses Logan
Mallory on Strike

Look out for:

Claudia and the Genius of Elm Street

JESSI'S WISH

Ann M. Martin

Scholastic Children's Books,
Scholastic Publications Ltd,
7-9 Pratt Street, London NW1 0AE

Scholastic Inc.,
555 Broadway, New York, NY 10012-3999, USA

Scholastic Canada Ltd,
123 Newkirk Road, Richmond Hill,
Ontario L4C 3G5, Canada

Ashton Scholastic Pty Ltd,
P O Box 579, Gosford, New South Wales,
Australia

Ashton Scholastic Ltd,
Private Bag 92801, Penrose,
Auckland, New Zealand

First published in the US by Scholastic Inc., 1991
First published in the UK by Scholastic Publications Ltd, 1994

Text copyright © Ann M. Martin, 1991
THE BABYSITTERS CLUB is a registered trademark of Scholastic Inc.

ISBN 0 590 55440 9

Typeset in Plantin by Contour Typesetters, Southall, London
Printed by Cox & Wyman Ltd, Reading, Berks.

10 9 8 7 6 5 4 3 2 1

*This book is for the real Danielle,
whose courage, strength, and optimism
make lots of wishes come true.
Thank you, Danielle.*

1st CHAPTER

"Whing, whing. Whing, whing."

That's Squirt-talk. It means, "Swing, swing. Swing, swing." Squirt is my baby brother. He doesn't say many words yet, but he loves swinging, so he made up a word for *that* pretty quickly.

I am Jessica Ramsey, known as Jessi. I'm eleven years old. My family and I live in Stoneybrook, Connecticut, a small town. We're sort of newcomers, since we arrived near the beginning of this school year, when I was starting the sixth grade. I have a mum and a dad; a sister, Rebecca; and of course Squirt. Both of my parents work. They like their jobs a lot. In fact, Dad likes his so much that when his company told him he was being transferred to the branch office in Stamford, Connecticut, he picked up and moved us Ramseys to Stoneybrook, which is near

1

Stamford. (We used to live in New Jersey.)

Rebecca is eight. Just as I go by the nickname Jessi, she goes by the nickname Becca. Becca is a great little sister. She has a sense of humour and a good imagination, although she's shy. Sometimes I think she's too sensitive. Maybe she needs to develop a thicker skin. On the other hand, if she weren't so sensitive, she might not be so kind and thoughtful. Here's an example of what makes Becca special. You know how most kids participate in some kind of after-school activity? Like sports or dance lessons or Brownies or Cub Scouts? Well, when Becca decided to try an activity for the first time, she joined the Kids-Can-Do-Anything Club at her school, Stoneybrook Elementary. The club (which the members refer to simply as the Kids Club) is for boys and girls aged eight, nine, and ten, and its purpose is to . . . help others. The kids think of ways to help out in the community. Then the two teachers, who volunteer their time to run the club, help the kids carry out their plans. The kids have done all sorts of things. They cleared up the rubbish on a patch of wasteground so the mayor could put a park there. They collected food for people who wouldn't have had a Thanksgiving otherwise. And now they were working on collecting new toys to give to the children's ward at the hospital. Becca always comes home from a Kids Club meeting with a huge smile on her face.

There are two other members of our household. One is Misty, our hamster. The other is Aunt Cecelia. She moved in to look after Squirt and to give us a hand when Mama went back to work. Becca and I used to call her Aunt Dictator. That was right after she moved in, when she didn't really understand my family. She was *so* strict and mean. But now she is much nicer, and we all get on pretty well. The one thing I don't like about Aunt Cecelia is that she still seems to think she's my babysitter. And I'm *already* a babysitter! Before Aunt Cecelia came, I was always looking after Becca and Squirt. Now I don't have the chance very often. Which is a shame because I love to babysit and (sorry for bragging) I'm really good at it. I'm good enough to be part of a business called the Babysitters Club.

Today, though, I *was* sitting. It was a weekday afternoon. Mama and Daddy were at work. And Aunt Cecelia had made plans with some friends. So I was in charge of Squirt. And as soon as Becca returned from her Kids Club meeting I would be in charge of her, too.

Squirt had stopped singing "Whing, whing." In fact, he held his arms out towards me. That meant he wanted to get out of the swing. I lifted him up and put him on the ground near our swing set.

3

"Come on, Squirt. Walk to me!" My brother is beginning to toddle around. It's a good thing he wears about nineteen nappies. They provide a nice cushion for when he suddenly sits on his bottom, which happens about every ten wobbly steps he takes.

"Da!" cried Squirt, and hurtled himself into my arms.

I heard a clank in our garage then and realized that Becca had come home from school. (The clank was the sound of the kickstand on her bicycle hitting the cement floor.) A few moments later, she rounded the corner into our back garden.

"Hi, Becca!" I called.

"Hi." Becca's eyes were downcast. She didn't smile. She didn't even greet Squirt, whom she loves as much as I do. (In case you're wondering, Squirt is not my brother's real name. His name is John Philip Ramsey, Jr. But when he was born in the Oakley, New Jersey, hospital, he was the smallest baby in the nursery. It was the hospital staff who first called him Squirt, and the name has stuck, even though Squirt isn't much of a squirt any more.)

"Is something wrong?" I asked Becca. "Something with the toy collection?"

Becca dropped her schoolbag on the ground and sat on the end of the slide. "No," she replied, "the toy collection is going really well. Bellair's gave us one

hundred dollars' worth of new toys."
(Bellair's is Stoneybrook's department
store.)

"That's great!" I exclaimed. "So why do
you look as if you've just lost your best
fr—?" I stopped talking. Maybe Becca *had*
just lost her best friend. Maybe she'd had a
row with Charlotte Johanssen. Having a
row with a friend is never fun, but for Becca
it would be a crushing blow. First of all, she
doesn't make friends easily. Second of all,
moving to Stoneybrook was difficult for my
family; not just because of who we left
behind in New Jersey (our relatives and
good friends), but because not everyone in
Stoneybrook accepted us in the beginning.
That was because my family is black, and
only a few black families live in Stoneybrook. People thought we were "different".
But now we've settled in and made friends.
However—had something happened between Becca and Charlotte?

"Did you and Char have a row?" I asked.

Becca looked shocked. "A row?" she
squeaked.

"Well, you're upset about something."

"Yes, but not Char. Or the toy collection.
It's the Kids Club." Becca sat on the
ground next to me, where I was playing
with Squirt. "We might not be able to have
the club any more. We might have to stop
it."

"How come?"

5

"Because Mrs Simon's husband is going on a really long trip, and she decided to go with him. So she has to leave school for a while. She can't find anyone who'll take her place at the club, and Mr Katz doesn't think he can run the club by himself." (Miss Simon and Mr Katz are the two teachers who volunteer their time with the Kids Club.)

"Becca, that's too bad," I said.

"I know." Becca's voice wavered and her lower lip quivered.

"Are you sure that's the only reason you're upset?" I asked, frowning.

My sister didn't answer me for a long time. When she did, her eyes filled with tears. "You know what Vanessa Pike told me today?" she asked.

"What?" (Vanessa is another Kids Club member. She's a year older than Becca.)

"That one of the girls in the hospital who'll be getting toys from our collection used to be a club member."

"Well, that's nice. She'll—" I started to say.

"No! It isn't nice at all!" Becca interrupted me. "That girl is nine, like Vanessa. Her name is Danielle Roberts, and she's been in the hospital ever since last summer because she has leukaemia. You know what that is?"

"Yes," I said softly. "It's cancer of the blood. Sort of. I mean, I think it's cancer of the things in your body that *form* blood."

"Right," said Becca. "*Cancer*. And she's only a year older than me."

"That's awful," I agreed. "But you know what? I'm pretty sure that lots of kinds of cancer can be cured now. Especially leukaemia."

"Really?"

"Yup. I mean, it's still a terrible disease to have, but lots of kids recover from it these days. There are so many new kinds of medicine and treatments. I bet Danielle—"

Becca interrupted me again. "Then how come she's still in hospital? She's been there a long time."

"She's busy getting better. I didn't say it's *easy* to fight cancer."

Becca nodded. Her eyes overflowed.

I put my arms around her. "I'm sorry you're upset," I said. Then I added, "It's scary to think that kids can get so ill, isn't it?"

Becca nodded again. "Am I going to get cancer?" she asked.

"I hope not. But we can't be sure about those things. You probably *won't* get cancer, though."

"Danielle did."

"I know. That's *one* person out of the whole of the fourth grade."

"Yeah," agreed Becca, drying her eyes. She sniffled. (Aunt Cecelia would have pulled a tissue out of her sleeve, but I let Becca be sloppy.)

"Isn't it nice to think that Danielle might get well?"

Becca actually smiled. "Yup. And it's nice to think of her having fun with the toys we collect. Bellair's gave us some dolls."

"Great!" I said.

Becca put Squirt back in the swing and began to push him gently.

Whing, whing!" called Squirt.

I stood up and leaned against our fence for a while. I watched Becca and Squirt. And my mind returned to the Kids Club. Would it really come to an end? I couldn't believe that no one else would volunteer to help Mr Katz until Miss Simon came back. The club is important to an awful lot of people. Not just to the ones who benefit from it, like the kids in hospital, but also to its members. I knew quite a lot of the members, too. Apart from Becca, Charlotte, and Vanessa, there were Nicky Pike (Vanessa's younger brother), and a group of other children the Babysitters Club sometimes takes care of. The kids were proud of their work. And they had fun at club meetings. They would really be disappointed if they couldn't continue their after-school activity. I'd be disappointed, too. The club had been terrific for Becca.

What could I do about the problem? I wondered. Sometimes I feel as if I'm practically an adult and I can do anything. At other times I feel like a little kid. That's one of the problems with being eleven. My best friend, Mallory Pike, would agree with that. (By the way, Mallory is the older sister of Nicky and Vanessa. There are eight Pike kids altogether!) Mal thinks being eleven is as frustrating as I do. Maybe I would give her a call. Or maybe I would call one of my other friends in the BSC. (That's how we club members refer to the Babysitters Club.) I would certainly have my choice of people to call. Here's a list of the other members of the club: Kristy Thomas, Claudia Kishi, Mary Anne Spier, Dawn Schafer, and Stacey McGill.

I was about to take my sister and brother inside so I could phone Mallory, when Squirt suddenly shrieked, "Who!" He was pointing to his feet.

"Hey, he's learned a new word!" exclaimed Becca. "I think *who* means *shoe*."

"Well, you two," I replied. "You and your *who*s come inside. I have to make a phone call."

2nd CHAPTER

I've thought a lot about what makes a best friend. I still don't have an answer. Among the girls in the BSC are several pairs of best friends. There's Mal and me, of course. There are Stacey and Claudia, Mary Anne and Dawn, and Mary Anne and Kristy. (Yes, Mary Anne has *two* best friends.) It looks to me as if best friends have some things in common, but not *every*thing. For instance, Mal and I are the same, yet different. Maybe that means that best friends need to have something in common but also need to find something in each other that's foreign or unusual or unexpected. (Opposites attract.) I'm not sure, though. Friendship can be complicated.

Take me. As I've said, I come from a pretty typical family—a mum, a dad, three kids and an aunt. My passion is ballet. (I take lessons at a special dance school, and I've even starred in some productions.) I'm black. Now take Mallory. She comes from an eight-kid family, her passion is writing, and she's white. We couldn't be more different, right? Wrong. Mal and I happen to have some common interests. We both love children and babysitting, (duh), and we *adore* reading, especially horse stories. Our favourite books are by Marguerite Henry. She wrote *Misty of Chincoteague* and *Stormy, Misty's Foal* and *Mustang, Wild Spirit of the West*. Mal and I even read *Brighty of the Grand Canyon*, despite the fact that it's about a mule, not a horse. We like mysteries, too. Not horror stories, but *gentle* mysteries like the Green Knowe books by L.M. Boston, or *Tom's Midnight Garden* by Philippa Pearce. Time-travel is always fascinating and mysterious.

Uh-oh. I am *way* off the subject. Let me tell you some more about Mal, so you can see the ways in which we're alike and different. Okay. I've said that she has seven brothers and sisters. They're all younger than she is. And three of them are identical *triplets*. They are Byron, Jordan, and Adam, who are ten. Next comes nine-year-old Vanessa, then eight-year-old Nicky, then seven-year-old Margo, and finally five-year-old Claire. (The Pikes have a pet hamster, just like we do, only their hamster is called Frodo, after the character in *Lord of the Rings* by J. R. R. Tolkein.)

When Mal isn't looking after her brothers and sisters or reading or babysitting or doing her homework, she's writing and drawing. Mal would like to write books for children one day, and maybe illustrate the books, too. Mal feels insecure about her appearance. (I don't worry much about mine. I think that as long as I have the body of a ballerina, I'm okay.) But Mal thinks her nose is too big, her hair is too red, and she has too many freckles. On top of all that, Mal wears a brace (the clear kind, at least) and glasses. Her parents refuse to let her get contact lenses. However, they *did* let her get her ears pierced—which prompted my parents to let me get mine pierced at the same time. Even so, Mal and I both think our parents treat us like infants (another reason eleven is such an awful age). They won't let us babysit at night unless we're sitting at our own houses. They won't let us dress as wildly as we'd like to. The Pikes won't even let Mallory get a nose job. ("Just wait till I make my first million," says Mal.)

At any rate, as you can see, Mal and I are similar *and* different.

So are Kristy Thomas and Mary Anne Spier.

Kristy and Mary Anne grew up right next door to each other. (Well, now neither of them lives in her old house, but they were next door neighbours until the summer before they started the eighth grade. That was when Kristy's mum, who'd been divorced, got remarried. Kristy was the first of the two of them to move away.) Kristy and Mary Anne actually look a bit alike. They're both short for their age, which is thirteen (Kristy's shorter), and they both have brown eyes and longish brown hair, which they often wear in ponytails. Neither one is a terribly trendy dresser. This is because Kristy couldn't care less about clothes, while Mary Anne's father can be strict about his daughter's wardrobe. Here is what Kristy almost always wears: jeans, trainers, a poloneck and a jumper, sometimes a T-shirt and a sweatshirt. She also has a baseball cap with a picture of a collie on it. Mary Anne's father *used* to make her wear all this boring stuff, like tartan dresses, or corduroy pinafore dresses with plain white blouses. Now he's relaxed enough to let Mary Anne buy her own clothes. But she's *not* allowed to wear tight jeans, or shirts with a lot of glitter, or anything Mr Spier thinks is "too revealing". Needless to say, she hasn't been allowed to get her ears pierced. (Kristy doesn't have pierced ears, either, but only because she doesn't *want* them. She thinks punching holes in her ears is gross.)

One thing that's totally different about

Mary Anne and Kristy is their personalities. Kristy is outgoing; Mary Anne is shy. Kristy sometimes runs off at the mouth (she doesn't intend to be rude; she just doesn't always think before she speaks). Mary Anne won't even talk unless she's with people who she feels comfortable with. Kristy is a tomboy who loves sports (she coaches a softball team for little kids), and doesn't have much use for boys, unless the boy is Bart Taylor, coach of a rival softball team; Mary Anne is sensitive (she cries at the drop of a hat) and romantic, and is the first of any of the BSC members to have a *steady* boyfriend.

Also, Kristy and Mary Anne come from pretty different backgrounds, in terms of family, but now (surprisingly) their family situations are similar. This is what I mean: Kristy was born into a family with a mum, a dad, and two brothers (Sam and Charlie). A few years later, her little brother, David Michael, came along, and not much later . . . her father ran out on the family. He just *left* one day. So it was up to Mrs Thomas to bring up Kristy and her brothers, and to provide for them. She did both things really well. The Thomas kids are all down-to-earth and, well, just *nice*. And Mrs Thomas got a good job at a company in Stamford. I'm not sure what she does, but I know she's considered very important in the business. Anyway, when Kristy was in the seventh grade her mum met and fell in love with this man called Watson Brewer. Watson (that's how Kristy refers to him) is a real *millionaire*. And after the wedding, he moved Kristy and her family across town to his mansion. Kristy gained a part-time stepbrother and stepsister in the process. They're part-time because they live with their father only on alternating weekends and on certain holidays. The rest of the time they live with their mother and stepfather, who have a house in Stoneybrook not far from Watson's. Since Kristy has absolutely fallen in love with Andrew and Karen (who are four and seven) she wishes they could spend more time with their father. But Kristy's household is something of a zoo as it is. Her mum and Watson adopted a little girl from Vietnam (Emily Michelle is about two and a half), and then Nannie, Kristy's grandmother, moved in to help look after Emily. Also, David has a dog, Watson has a cat, and Karen and Andrew keep two goldfish at their dad's. Whew!

Mary Anne, on the other hand, was born to her mum and her dad, but she has no brothers and sisters. Then, when Mary Anne was really little, her mum died. (Mary Anne doesn't really remember her mother.) After that, it was just Mary Anne and her father, on their own. Mr Spier loved his daughter, but he was pretty strict with her. I think he wanted to prove that he could bring up a perfect child all by himself. He made Mary Anne wear clothes that *he* chose for her, he made her wear her hair in plaits, he wouldn't let her talk on the phone after dinner, and so forth. Then everything changed.

In January of the seventh grade, Dawn Schafer moved to town. Her mother had grown up in Stoneybrook, so after she and Dawn's dad decided to get a divorce, she moved back here from California. And Mrs Schafer and Mr Spier began to see each other, and finally got *married*. Mary Anne and Dawn, who were already close friends, became stepsisters. The Spiers moved into the old farmhouse Mrs Schafer had bought, and suddenly Mary Anne had a much bigger family—a father, a stepmother, a stepsister, and a stepbrother. (I'll tell you about Jeff, her stepbrother, in a few minutes.) Oh, and Tigger, her kitten. This was quite a change, but Mary Anne likes her new family—most of the time.

You must be curious about Dawn by now, since she's Mary Anne's sister as well as one of her best friends. Let's see. Dawn and her younger brother, Jeff, were born in California. They lived there until the divorce. Then they moved to Connecticut with their mum. As you can imagine, this was sort of a shock for them, moving right across the country—and leaving sunny

California for a snowy Connecticut winter. They also left their father, of course, which turned out to be especially hard on Jeff. Long before his mother and Mary Anne's father decided to get married, Jeff moved *back* to California. He simply couldn't adjust to his new life. Now he lives happily with his dad. Tough as the past couple of years have been, Dawn has accepted things well. She seems happy with her new life and her family, partly, maybe, because she gets to visit California pretty often. But mostly, that's just how Dawn is. She's practical and calm, which is good for Mary Anne, and she's also very much an individual. She dresses the way she likes, no matter what other people are wearing, and she eats the way she likes—which is healthy. Dawn doesn't eat meat or sweets. What she likes are fruits and vegetables and a few weird things such as tofu and bean sprouts.

Dawn and Mary Anne have got along well from the moment they first met. Mary Anne is as accepting as Dawn is. Dawn is quieter than Kristy, and she and Mary Anne share a love of reading and of certain films. (Dawn especially likes ghost stories, which is interesting because in her house is a *secret passage* . . . which may be haunted.)

All right. On to Stacey and Claudia, the last pair of best friends. Boy, are they different from anyone else in the club! They are *so* sophisticated. It's hard to believe they're the same age as Kristy, Dawn, and Mary Anne, and only two years older than Mallory and me. Somehow, Stacey seems even more sophisticated than Claud. I suppose that's because she grew up in big, glamorous New York City. She lived there until the summer before the seventh grade. Then she and her parents (Stacey is an only child) moved to Connecticut when, just like with my family, the company her dad works for transferred his job to Stamford. Stacey liked Connecticut, and straight away, she and Claudia met and became friends. The McGills had been living in Stoneybrook for less than a year when guess what. Mr McGill's company transferred him *back* to New York. So Stacey and her parents left Stoneybrook. (Want to hear something weird? When the McGills sold their house, *my family* bought it! We live in Stacey's former home. In fact, my bedroom used to be Stacey's.) Anyway, while the McGills were in New York for the second time, something sad happened. Stacey's parents decided to get a divorce. Almost as bad, Mr McGill wanted to remain in New York City because of his job, while Mrs McGill wanted to return to Stoneybrook, which she had liked very much—and Stacey was left with a dilemma. Where did she want to live (and with which parent?) The decision was hers to make, and it was a tough one. At last Stacey chose to move back to Connecticut with her mother, but she thinks she's hurt her father's feelings.

Life hasn't been easy for Stacey McGill. Apart from her family problems, she's got a physical problem, a disease called diabetes. Diabetics don't process sugar properly, which can mess up their blood sugar level. Unfortunately, Stacey has a severe form of diabetes (she's called a brittle diabetic), and not only has to stay on a strict, calorie-counting, no-sweets diet, but has to give herself injections of something called insulin every day. (Ugh!)

Despite these things, Stacey has emerged as one of the coolest kids in all of SMS. She dresses in *really* cool clothes—leggings, cowboy boots, hats, short skirts, a lot of black, etc. She has blonde hair, which her mother lets her perm every now and then, and, of course, her ears are pierced. (By the way, speaking of pierced ears, did I mention that Dawn has had each of her ears pierced *twice*?) Stacey's are pierced the usual way, like Mal's and mine.

Claudia's aren't. Claudia Kishi, who I suppose is the funkiest dresser of all us BSC members, has had one of her ears pierced once and the other twice. Her clothes are similar to Stacey's, but I suppose that if Claudia were to offer a fashion tip, it would be, "Accessorize to the max." She certainly follows her own advice, wearing tons of hats, belts, boots, jewellery (she makes a lot of her own jewellery), and hair ornaments. Claud has beautiful, long, black hair, which she wears in different styles. She's really striking-looking. Her parents are Japanese, and Claud's features are exotic. Also—despite a passion for junk food—her complexion is perfect.

Claud is . . . I was about to say she's a real character, but I suppose what I mean is that she's fascinating, at least to me. Her bedroom says a lot about her. It's full of hidden things—the junk food her parents disapprove of, and the Nancy Drew mysteries she loves to read but which her parents also disapprove of. And it is cluttered with art materials. Claudia is a *really* talented artist. Not only does she make jewellery, but she paints, draws, sculpts, throws pots (that means she creates pottery), and more. Some of her work has been awarded prizes. This is good for Claud because she's not much of a student—but her older sister, Janine, is a genius. Luckily Claud is recognized for her artwork, since Janine sweeps the board in the academic category.

Claud was born and raised in Stoneybrook, and she and Janine live with their parents (no pets). You can see that while Claud and Stacey are wild (even daring) and outgoing, their families and backgrounds are quite different, which only goes to back up my half-formed theory about best friends.

I realized that I'd been staring at the kitchen phone for about five minutes, while my mind wandered. I shook my head. Then I reached for the receiver. I was just about to call Mallory when . . .

"Who!" cried Squirt, and I looked at his feet and saw that one shoe was missing.

I had to go on a shoe hunt before I could phone Mal.

3rd
CHAPTER

I didn't reach Mal until that evening. But I was glad I finally did. Mal is so practical. She said, "Why don't you talk about the Kids Club at the next BSC meeting?"

What a simple, wonderful suggestion. Of course I should mention the Kids Club to my friends. They always have good ideas. Especially Kristy. She's the Queen of Good Ideas.

In fact, without Kristy, there wouldn't be a Babysitters Club at all. . . . What *is* the Babysitters Club? Well, for those of you who don't know, the BSC is a very successful sitting business that my friends and I run here in Stoneybrook. One reason the business is so successful is the official way in which we conduct ourselves. The BSC meets regularly, and each member has a special job or role in the club.

The club began a while ago—before

Dawn and I even lived in Stoneybrook. And when Mal was young enough to still be a babysit*ee*, not yet a babysitter. Everything started with Kristy. Back when she, Claudia, Stacey, and Mary Anne were just beginning the seventh grade (and when Stacey had just moved to Connecticut for the first time), Kristy, her mum, and her brothers were living in their old house opposite Claudia and next door to Mary Anne. Mrs Thomas had only been seeing Watson Brewer for a short time. And David Michael was just six years old. Charlie, Sam, and Kristy were supposed to take turns watching him after school (until Mrs Thomas came home from work), but they lead busy lives, so every now and then a day would come along when none of them was free to take care of their little brother. Then Mrs Thomas would have to rush to arrange a babysitter. One evening, Kristy was watching her mum make one call after another, trying to find an available sitter, when she got her best idea ever. Her mother would save a lot of time if she could make just one phone call—and reach a whole lot of sitters at once.

And that was the beginning of the Babysitters Club. As soon as she could, Kristy told Mary Anne and Claudia about her idea, and they decided to meet several times a week. If people who needed babysitters called them during meetings, they'd reach *three* capable sitters. Mary Anne and Claudia loved the idea but thought they needed a fourth member. Claud suggested Stacey, with whom she was just becoming friends. So Stacey met Kristy and Mary Anne and was made the fourth member of the BSC.

The club was a success from the beginning. I think this was for two reasons. One, Kristy knows how to advertise. Two, Kristy is the perfect club chairman, since she also knows how to run things. Why was advertising so important in the beginning? Because that's how people learned about the BSC. The club members had decided to meet on Monday, Wednesday, and Friday afternoons from five-thirty until six. But how would anyone else know that? They made up leaflets and distributed them in the neighbourhood. They placed an ad in the local paper. And they told everyone they could think of about their new business.

What a success! By the middle of that school year, when Dawn moved to town, the girls were doing so much business that they needed a fifth club member. And later, when Stacey had moved back to New York, she was replaced by both Mal (who was finally old enough to sit) and me. Of course, after her parents' divorce, when Stacey returned to Stoneybrook, she rejoined the club immediately. We have seven members now (plus two associate members whom I'll describe later) and I think that's enough!

Remember when I said that Kristy is the perfect chairman? This is why: besides deciding that the club should meet three times a week and that we should advertise our services, she decided that everyone should have certain responsibilities, or hold a certain position in the club. So Kristy became the chairman. (After all, the BSC was her idea.) As chairman, she's responsible for running things smoothly, and for continuing to come up with great ideas. Here are some of her ideas:

—To keep a club notebook. The notebook is more of a diary. Kristy insists that each of us write up every single job we go on, and that we read everyone's entries once a week. I'll tell you something. Most of us do *not* like writing in that diary. It's boring. But—we all like *reading* the notebook. Now *that's* interesting. We find out what happened when our friends were sitting, how they solved sticky sitting situations, and what's going on with the families we sit for regularly. (It's always helpful to know if a child has developed a new fear, has been ill, is having trouble at school, *or* if a child has a new interest, has done well at something, has a new friend, etc.)

—To keep a club record book containing information about the clients of the BSC. For instance, their names, addresses, and phone numbers, the ages of their kids, and the rates they pay. Also included in the record book are the appointment pages, where Mary Anne (the club secretary) schedules all of our jobs; and a section where Stacey (the club treasurer) records how much money we earn while sitting.

—To create Kid-Kits. Here is Kristy at her brilliant best! Kristy took a simple idea (that, for whatever reason, kids like playing with other people's toys better than their own), and turned it into, well, another great idea. A Kid-Kit is a box (we each have one) that we fill with our own (old) games, books, and toys, as well as some new things that have to be replaced from time to time, such as crayons and other art materials, colouring books, sticker books, etc. We sometimes take the kits with us when we babysit. They're great for rainy days, for entertaining new sitting charges, and sometimes for absolutely no special reason! The kids love Kid-Kits, so when their parents come home, they find happy faces, which makes them more likely to call the BSC the next time they need a sitter.

Whew! Sometimes Kristy's brain is hard to keep up with.

Okay. On to the vice-chairman of the BSC. That's Claudia. She gets to be vice-chairman because we hold our meetings in her bedroom. Her room was chosen because Claud has her own telephone *and* her own phone number. This is important (and lucky). During our meetings we spend a lot of time on the phone. It's nice to know that when we use Claud's phone, we aren't tying up some adult's line for half an hour three times a week. Claud is very generous—with her room, her phone, and her junk food (club snacks). She deserves to be vice-chairman.

As I mentioned before, Mary Anne is our secretary. This is a fairly complicated task. In order to schedule sitting jobs, Mary Anne has to keep track of my ballet lessons, Claud's art classes, Mal's orthodontist appointments, Stacey's weekends with her father, etc. Then she records our jobs on the appointment pages. That's not easy. She's also in charge of keeping the information in the record book up-to-date.

In fact, Mary Anne is in charge of the entire record book—except for one section. That section is Stacey's, where, as our treasurer, she makes a list of the money we earn. This is just for our information. Each of us gets to keep all the money from every job we take. (We don't try to divide up the money or anything.) We do, however, have to contribute club subs at the Monday meetings. We all hate parting with our money, but subs are important. Stacey puts the money in our treasury (a manila envelope) and doles it out as needed. We spend subs money on lots of things. We use it to buy more items for the Kid-Kits. We use it to help pay Claud's phone bill. We use it to pay Charlie Thomas to drive Kristy to and from meetings now that she no longer lives in the neighbourhood. And sometimes we use it for something fun, such as food for a BSC sleepover. Stacey is a good treasurer because she's an excellent maths pupil. (She actually *likes* maths.)

Dawn is called an alternate officer, which is like being an understudy in a play. She knows the duties and responsibilities of every club member, so she can fill in if someone has to miss a meeting. (When Stacey temporarily moved back to New York, Dawn became the treasurer. She gladly gave up that job when Stacey returned. She couldn't stand our grumbling each time she collected subs. Besides, she hates maths.)

Guess what Mallory and I are in charge of. Nothing. Well, I don't really mean *nothing*. We're good babysitters. It's just that because we're eleven, and the unfortunate product of overprotective parents, we're not allowed to sit at night (unless we're sitting for our own brothers and sisters). Mostly, we sit after school and on weekend days. Because of this, we are the club's junior officers. Sometimes I feel a little unimportant, since when Mal or I miss a meeting, Dawn doesn't have to do anything to replace us. However, Kristy assures us that we're necessary. Without Mal and me to take on so many daytime jobs, she says, she and the older club members would have to turn down some of the evening jobs.

I know that makes us sound busy, and we are. (Busy, I mean.) We're busy enough so that we had to sign on those two associate members I told you about earlier. An associate member doesn't come to club meetings but is a reliable sitter we can call on in case a job is offered to the club that *none* of us full-time members can take. You'd think that with seven people and seven schedules, that wouldn't happen. But it does. Occasionally. And when it does, we offer the job to one of our associates. (That way, we don't have to disappoint our clients.) Our associate members are Shannon Kilbourne, a friend of Kristy's who lives in her new neighbourhood, and Logan Bruno. Logan is Mary Anne's boyfriend!

This is how a typical club meeting starts. My friends and I trickle into Claud's room between five-fifteen and five-thirty. I usually arrive dangerously close to five-thirty. That's because often I rush to a club meeting after I've had a ballet lesson in Stamford.

Kristy is always sitting in Claud's director's chair, wearing a visor, a pencil stuck behind one ear. This is her Chairman's Look. She keeps an eye on the digital clock, which is our official club timekeeper. As

29

soon as those numbers turn from 5:29 to 5:30, Kristy is on the case. She sits up straight, trying to appear as tall as possible. Then she says, "Any club business?" This is the clue for Stacey to collect subs (if it's Monday). It's also the time for us to raise questions or to talk about problems. Usually these are babysitting questions or problems. But not always.

The day after Becca came home with her sad news about the Kids Club, I was still thinking about Mr Katz and Miss Simon. When Kristy said, "Any club business?" I cleared my throat.

"Yes, Jessi?" said Kristy.

"I've been thinking. You know the Kids Club?" I began. Everyone nodded, so I explained what was happening.

"That's pretty rotten," Kristy commented when I had finished talking.

"Yeah. Nicky and Vanessa are really upset," added Mallory.

"So's Becca," I said. "And that's what I was thinking about. There must be *some* way to keep the club going."

"I can't believe no one will volunteer to take Miss Simon's place," said Dawn.

"Me, neither. . . . But I have this idea."

"What?" asked Mary Anne.

"I could take Miss Simon's place."

Silence.

"I want to help out," I began.

"Jessi, what *aren't* you telling us?" said Kristy.

"My idea. I haven't told you the whole idea yet. This is—oh, all right. I'll just say it. I thought that maybe, instead of baby-sitting for the next month or so, we could do some volunteer work. I'd really like to help with the Kids Club."

I had absolutely no idea how the other members of the BSC were going to react to this. Mal and I don't usually make major suggestions, us being junior members and all. It occurred to me that Kristy might kill me.

I didn't dare look up. But after a few moments of silence, Mal poked me in the ribs. "What?" I asked her. And *then* I looked up.

Everyone was grinning.

"That," said Stacey, "is a terrific idea. You know what my mum was telling me the other day? She said that a diabetes clinic is going to open soon in Stoneybrook. And they're looking for kids or teenagers with diabetes who will meet kids who've just been diagnosed, and talk to them and give them advice and stuff. I'd like to do that. I wish someone had talked to *me* when I first got ill."

"I bet we could all find something to do," said Kristy.

"Maybe I could teach art!" exclaimed Claud.

"What about the club, though?" asked Dawn, frowning. "We can't run the BSC *and* volunteer, can we? I mean, I want to help out, but . . ."

"We'll think of something," said Kristy, who was obviously too excited to think straight about anything. Her mind was running in a zillion directions. "I wonder if I could help out in the class for special kids at school. Or, remember when we babysat for Susan?" (Susan's family lives not far from Claud. Susan has a disorder called autism.) "Maybe I could work with autistic kids somehow. Or, wait! I could tutor! Let's see. What subject am I really good at? Okay, you lot. We have a mission. I call an emergency club meeting for Saturday afternoon. By then, we all should have looked into places that need volunteers."

Wow! I had sent us on a mission!

4th CHAPTER

"Thank you for saving my life," said Becca dramatically.

I smiled. "Any time."

"You know what this means?" asked my sister. "It means that now we won't be even until *I've* saved *your* life."

"With any luck, it won't need to be saved," I replied.

Goodness. You'd think I'd pulled Becca from a burning building or an overturned car. But this was all I'd done: I'd met Becca at her school after the next meeting of the Kids Club, and I'd talked to Mr Katz.

"What are *you* doing here?" asked Becca, when she saw me. She wasn't expecting me, and she usually walks home by herself or with Charlotte after a meeting.

"Charming!" I answered, but I wasn't really annoyed. "I just want to see Mr Katz

33

for a few minutes. If you and Char wait outside, I'll walk home with you."

"Okay," replied Becca, looking puzzled.

I stepped inside the large room where the Kids Club meets. Mr Katz was busy putting art materials in a cabinet.

"Excuse me," I said, feeling timid. "Mr Katz?"

He turned round. "Yes?"

"Um, I'm Jessi Ramsey . . . Becca Ramsey's sister!"

Mr Katz smiled. "Jessi," he said warmly. "I've heard a lot about you from Becca and Charlotte. And several other pupils here. You're a babysitter?"

"Yes." I explained about the BSC. Then I said, "Becca told me about Miss Simon. I'm really sorry. I'm sorry about the club, too. Disbanding it would be awful. The kids would be pretty upset."

"Well—"

"So I was wondering," I rushed on. "Could I help out? I know I'm only eleven, and I know I can't take Miss Simon's place, but I'd like—"

"It's volunteer work, Jessi," Mr Katz interrupted me. "We don't get paid."

"Oh, that's okay. I mean, I'm used to getting paid when I babysit, but this is important to me. And I understand that when Miss Simon comes home, she'll probably want her job back. That's okay, too. I don't want to leave the Babysitters Club permanently."

"I don't know what to say," exclaimed Mr Katz. He paused. "How about a trial period to see how this works out? It has to be right for you, too."

"That sounds great."

Mr Katz and I agreed that I would give him a hand at the next four meetings of the Kids Club. If we were happy—and if the kids were happy—then I would stay on until Miss Simon returned, which might be as soon as a month.

And this was what prompted Becca to say I'd saved her life. She could hardly believe that the Kids Club might survive after all.

"It's no guarantee," I warned her.

"I know. But it's two more weeks. Besides, you'll be great, Jessi!"

"It'll definitely be fun," I agreed.

I was prepared for the Saturday emergency meeting of the BSC.

Kristy had called the special meeting for two o'clock in the afternoon. I suppose everyone was as excited as I was about what we were going to be doing, because by one-thirty, the entire BSC had gathered in Claud's room and Kristy had called the meeting to order.

I looked round at my friend's faces. Everyone was beaming—Kristy, poised in the director's chair; Dawn, sitting backwards in Claud's wooden desk chair, her chin resting on the top rung of the back; Mary Anne, Claud, and Stacey, in a row on Claud's bed; and Mal and I, sitting cross-legged on the floor. I waited expectantly for Kristy to speak.

"Okay," she said, grinning. "I have a feeling I don't really need to ask this question, but did everyone here look into volunteering?"

"Yes!" we replied. (We wouldn't have turned up so early otherwise.)

"Great. Well, let's just take turns talking about what we found out. . . . I'll start. I mean, I *am* the chairman." (As if we could forget.) "Okay. There were so many things I could have done. Tutoring, teaching, I asked about the Big Sister organization. But then I remembered the day-care centre in town. David Michael used to go there. Before he started school. It's a pretty nice place. It's for kids whose parents work. There's a programme for babies, one for toddlers, one for nursery school kids, and there's even an after-school programme for kids up to ten. I remembered that they need volunteer helpers. So I signed up. I start next week."

"Cool," said Stacey. "What will you be doing?"

"I'm not sure exactly. I think I just observe at first. Or maybe I help out wherever I'm needed. I'll know more on Wednesday." Kristy turned to Dawn. "Your turn," she said.

Dawn straightened up. "I'm going to spend three afternoons each week at the Baker Institute. It's in Stamford, but that's okay. They provide transportation for the kids from Stoneybrook who use the institute, so I'll just travel with them after school and come back with them at dinnertime. I can help out on the bus while I'm on it."

"What's the Baker Institute?" I asked.

"It's a programme for kids who are physically disabled. Most of them are in wheelchairs. They have cerebral palsy and muscular dystrophy and things. When they're at Baker they get physiotherapy and they can take part in lots of activities—art, creative writing, music, all kinds of things."

I had about a million questions (such as, "What's muscular dystrophy?"), but Kristy had already gone on to Stacey.

"Did you find out about the diabetes clinic?" she asked.

"Yup," said Stace. "I talked to my mum straight away. She was really pleased that I want to volunteer. She gave me the name of the director, and I had a meeting with her the next afternoon. The clinic hasn't even opened yet, but already there's a long list of people who have signed up for various programmes. One of the programmes is the one I told you about. Kids like me will talk to other kids who've recently found out they're diabetic. The director—her name is Miss Arnell—told me about two kids, an eight-year-old boy and a ten-year-old girl, who've just been diagnosed. I'm supposed to phone them and talk to them and then spend some time with them. I think it'll be interesting but maybe hard. I remember how scared I was when the doctor first told me I had diabetes."

It came as no surprise to any of us that Claud was going to help teach an art class, as she'd hoped she might.

"It's at the community centre," Claud explained. "They offer a lot of art classes. This is an after-school one for seven-year-olds—"

"Wait a sec," interrupted Mallory. "When does it meet?"

"Tuesday and Friday afternoons."

Mallory began to laugh. "I think Margo's taking that class."

"Great!" exclaimed Claud.

"Here's more good news," said Kristy. "I think Karen's signed up, too!"

"I'll be prepared," said Claud.

Mary Anne was going to be doing something different from the rest of us. "I won't be working at an organization or a community centre," she began. "You see, my dad and Dawn's mum are friends with a couple who have a little boy who's brain damaged. They need people to come over to their house and work with their son, and help out with their two other kids. I think Frankie—that's the boy—is almost a full-time job."

Mal was next. "There's a recreation programme at the park," she said. "It's free. Kids can be part of it whenever they want to —after school, at weekends. All they have to do is show up. The counsellors offer sports, and arts and crafts. Sometimes the triplets go. It's really nice for kids to have something to do. But the counsellors need help."

I only spoke briefly. Everyone knew what I was going to say. After all, the Kids Club was what had started our "mission".

"This is really great," said Kristy, after I'd talked about meeting Mr Katz. "There's just one thing."

"Uh-oh. What?" said Stacey.

"What Dawn said before. Our regular clients. Club meetings. We still have to decide what we're going to do for the next month or so. I don't want to sound . . . you know. But we worked so hard to make our club successful. What if we put ourselves out of business?"

I almost told Kristy she was overreacting, until I thought about the problem. We *had* worked hard to be successful. People relied on us. They expected to be able to reach us during meetings.

"Wait a sec," spoke up Claud. "I know we're going to be busy, but the club doesn't have to *stop*. We have associate members, you know. Anyhow, we won't all be working seven days a week. My art class is on Tuesdays and Fridays. I can answer the phone on Mondays and Wednesdays."

"I could answer it on Fridays," I said.

We agreed to continue our meetings. Whoever could show up, would show up. We'd just have to be extra careful about scheduling jobs. And we'd have to rely on Logan and Shannon more than usual. (Kristy phoned them to make sure they didn't mind. And they didn't.)

"Well," said Kristy, getting to her feet, "next week should be interesting. I think this change will be good for us."

"And for a lot of other people," I added.

5th CHAPTER

The room was crowded. And noisy. Sixteen kids can be awfully loud. Especially when school has finished, and they're hungry and excited and I don't know what else. I tried to remember how it felt to be eight years old and at the end of a school day.

Was I supposed to be doing anything? I looked around the room.

Nicky Pike was standing on a chair, yelling to another boy to toss him this trainer they were playing with. (I don't know who the trainer belonged to. All the kids were wearing their shoes.)

In the back of the room, Vanessa Pike and two girls were practising cheers they'd seen the high school cheerleaders perform.

Two other girls were chasing a boy round the room. The boy tripped over a chair and fell—and the girls tackled him. "Cowabunga!" they yelled.

In the midst of all this, my sister was sitting at a desk. Charlotte Johanssen was sitting next to her. The two of them were poring over something in one of their schoolbooks. They weren't even aware of the pandemonium that surrounded them. They must have great powers of concentration.

So must Mr Katz. He was leaning against the teacher's desk, flipping through some sheets of paper. He didn't even notice when the trainer sailed across the room and smacked into the blackboard behind him. Were the kids in the Kids Club always this wild? Becca had never said anything about that. On the other hand, maybe she'd never noticed.

I approached Mr Katz. "Hi," I said.

He looked up quickly. "Jessi. Hi. I'm glad you're here. Welcome to . . ." (he glanced around the wild room) ". . . the Kids Club. Don't worry. They won't be this noisy all afternoon. They just need to let off some steam before we start. It's been a long day."

I nodded. (I understood why Becca liked Mr Katz so much.)

Mr Katz let the kids run around for about five more minutes. Then he clapped his hands and called, "Okay!"

That was all it took.

Every single kid in the room stopped whatever he or she was doing and scrambled for a spot on the floor. (The desks had been pushed against the wall in one corner of the room, and the kids crowded into this space.)

What was I supposed to do? Sit with the children? Stand with Mr Katz?

Mr Katz answered the questions for me. He put his hand on my shoulder and said, "Okay, everybody. Settle down. I'm glad you came this afternoon. As you know, Miss Simon is out of town for a while. She hopes to be back in a month or so. Meanwhile, something fortunate has happened. I want you to meet Jessi Ramsey. This is Becca's sister. She's offered to give us a hand until Miss Simon returns. Jessi will be here to answer questions and to do anything Miss Simon would have done—except drive our van." (The kids giggled.)

Mr Katz turned to me. "Jessi, I expect you know a lot of the kids here. In case you see some unfamiliar faces, though, I'm going to ask everyone to introduce himself or herself to you."

The children took turns saying their names aloud. (When it was Becca's turn, she giggled and said, "I'm your sister. I think you know me.")

Then Mr Katz got down to business. He picked up the papers he'd been looking through a few moments before. "Guess what," he said. "You lot have got some post."

The kids, who were already paying attention, seemed to perk up even more."

"Who'd we get post from?" asked Nicky Pike.

"I'll read one of the letters to you. You can see for yourselves," replied Mr Katz. He sorted through the papers, chose one, and read, " 'Dear Kids Club, Thank you for the great toys. They are great. We are having a great time with them. Sometimes the nurses let us choose a toy from the playroom and bring it to our room for the night. That is great! I always choose the panda bear. Thank you. Sincerely, John.' "

"The kids at the hospital!" exclaimed Charlotte Johanssen. She had raised her hand (and she left it raised while she spoke), but she hadn't waited to be called on. Mr Katz didn't seem to care. "The kids got the toys. I suppose they like them," continued Charlotte.

"Read some more letters!" called out a boy whose name (I thought) was Bruce.

"Okay." Mr Katz shifted his weight from one foot to the other. "Let's see. Here we go. 'Dear Kids Club, Hi! I broke my arm. I broke it playing football with my brothers. It wasn't their fault, though. Thank you very much for sending the toys. I only have to stay in hospital for a few days. But I really appreciate the toys. They help pass the time. Love, Abbie.' "

"Abbie!" cried Nicky. "You mean a *girl* was playing football?"

"Girls can play football, too," said Vanessa.

Mr Katz ignored this. "Here's an interesting letter," he said. " 'Dear Kids Club, Thank you, thank you, thank you for all the wonderful toys. We really needed them. I feel as if I have been in hospital all my life! But guess what. The chemo is working. I can come home soon. I look funny, but I don't care. I can't wait to go back to school. Honest! I used to love being absent from school. Now I hope I never have to miss another day. We have Nintendo at the hospital. And a VCR. The video lady brings good films. Oh! I should tell you what my favourite new toy is. Well, it's not really a toy. It's the art materials that Witherspoon's donated. I have been making jewellery. I wasn't going to mention this, but I decided maybe I should warn you. The chemo made most of my hair fall out. Don't worry. I won't make you look at a bald head. I'll get a scarf or a wig. I can't wait to see you. Thanks again! Love . . .' " Mr Katz paused.

The room was silent.

Finally someone whispered, "Danielle?"

Mr Katz nodded.

Becca's eyes met mine. I thought she might cry. Instead she said slowly, "Those kids sound like they need pen pals. We'd better read the rest of the letters."

Mr Katz smiled at her. "Is that going to be your next project?"

The kids still looked a little stunned. After a few moments, Vanessa raised her hand.

"Yes?" said Mr Katz.

"I thought we were going to pick up litter."

"Gross," said Bruce. "We've just cleared up that place for the park. I'm tired of litter."

A few kids laughed. The tension eased. Mr Katz perched himself on the edge of the teacher's desk, so I did the same thing.

Wendy Jervis raised her hand. "Arts and crafts—" she began.

"Wendy!" exclaimed Peter Tiegreen. "Can't you think about something else besides art?"

"But we were going to make presents, and the people who deliver Meals on Wheels were going to give them to all the people who can't leave their homes."

The kids turned to Mr Katz and me. They seemed to be saying, "Help us make up our minds!"

"You *do* need to decide on a new project," said Mr Katz.

The children listened to him seriously. I was impressed by how quickly they'd calmed down and by how attentive they were. But then, that made sense. They weren't at the club meeting because they *had* to be. They were there because they *wanted* to be. They liked thinking up new projects, other ways to help people.

"You did a terrific job with the toy collection," Mr Katz went on. "But it's over now. Well, except for these letters."

Mr Katz was interrupted by my sister. "Who here has ever been in hospital?" she asked. (About half the kids raised their hands.) "Wouldn't you have liked to have a pen pal then? Especially if you had to stay in the hospital a really long time . . . like Danielle?"

I wanted to hug my sister. I was so proud of her. But I did just what Mr Katz was doing, which was waiting for someone to respond to her.

"I think", spoke up Vanessa Pike, "that we should at least answer those letters. The kids would like to get post. *We* liked getting *their* letters."

"Let's hear another letter," said Charlotte to Mr Katz.

"All right." He chose one. " 'Dear Kids Club, The toys are so cool! Thank you! I have been in hospital for almost a month. This is the third time I've been here this year. I have cystic fibrosis. I am *always* in hospital. It's hard to make friends here. Kids come and go. Danielle says she knows you. She's my friend, too. But she's going home soon. She's so lucky.' "

"Lucky?" cried Wendy. "She has leukaemia!"

"I think the hospital is a pretty lonely place," said Becca pointedly.

I expected Wendy to make a face at my sister. But she just stopped talking.

Mr Katz finished reading the letter. He placed it on the desk. "You've received eleven letters altogether," he told the kids.

"And there are sixteen of us," said my sister, taking charge. "So six people can write letters by themselves, and the rest of us will find a partner and answer the letters in teams."

"Let's look at *all* the letters," said Nicky.

"Why? Are you afraid to write to a girl?" teased Vanessa.

"*No*," said Nicky so fast that I was sure that was exactly what he'd meant.

Mr Katz handed the letters round, and the kids read them eagerly.

"Hey!" cried a girl whose name I'd forgotten. "Maybe they'd like pictures of us. You know, so they can *see* who the letters are from."

"Do you still have your Polaroid camera, Mr Katz?" asked Bruce.

"It's in the cabinet," he replied.

"Goody!" exclaimed Nicky. "We can

take funny pictures, too."

The kids were moving around now. Some were swapping letters, some had followed Mr Katz to the cabinet, some were getting out paper and pencils.

"We could decorate the paper and make beautiful stationery," I heard Charlotte say to Becca, and I knew they were going to work together.

I started towards them, but their heads were bent as they whispered together. They didn't look as though they needed any help.

Don't favour Becca, I told myself. And remember that the Kids Club is *her* club. This is her territory. Don't interfere.

I took my own advice.

Anyway, *other* kids needed me. "Jessi?" said Wendy. "How do you spell 'hospital'?"

Bruce pulled at my hand as I walked past. "Can you take my photo?" he asked.

"*I'll* take your photo," said another boy. "We're partners."

"How about if I take a photo of you together?" I asked.

"Yes!" cried Bruce. "No, wait! Take two. A silly one and a nice one."

"Photo limit!" said Mr Katz then. "One per person. The film is expensive."

"We'd better be careful, then," said Bruce.

"Jessi, you can only take two. No repeats. Okay. This will be the serious one."

The boys posed, as if for a school photograph. Then they stuck out their tongues and crossed their eyes. But they didn't laugh.

"I wonder if he'll like these pictures," said Bruce's friend.

"I wonder if you can get well from cystic fibrosis," said Bruce.

6th CHAPTER

Wednesday

I used to go with my mum sometimes when she'd take David Michael to the day-care centre, or when she'd pick him up after work. But I suppose I'd forgotten a few things. Like how it must feel to be three years old at four o'clock in the afternoon when you've been in day care since seven in the morning and... you've missed your naps. Both of them. Or what it must feel like to be given the opportunity to... finger paint. Or what it must feel like when your mum or dad finally comes to pick you up....

I think Kristy had something of a shock on her first afternoon at the centre. She'd visited it recently, of course, but sitting in an armchair in the director's office is a bit different from trying to entertain a bunch of grumpy three-year-olds, or trying to read to a group of wriggly five-year-olds, or trying to feed eight babies at the same time.

The day-care centre is big. There's a room full of high chairs and toys for the babies, and another room for them to sleep in. There's a nap room for the older children, a playroom for the toddlers, another for the nursery school kids, another for the five- and six-year-olds, *another* for the seven- and eight-year-olds, and a study room for the oldest kids, and anyone else who needs it. There's a small gym, an arts-and-crafts room, a kitchen, a sick room, and outdoors, a playground. Until about three o'clock, when the older children are at school, the centre is less busy. Just after three, though, the school kids begin to come by for the afternoon programme. They can work on art projects, do their homework, play with their friends or their brothers and sisters, play in the playground, or help out with the younger children.

Wednesday was Kristy's first day at the centre. She arrived as soon after school as she could. She went straight to the director's office.

"Kristy. Hi. I'm so glad you're here," said Mrs Hall. "We've got a full house today, but we're a little understaffed. Where would you like to work?"

"Well..." Kristy was unprepared for the question. She'd thought Mrs Hall would assign her to an age group or to a certain room.

"Would you just like to float around today?" asked Mrs Hall. "You could help out wherever you're needed and also get acquainted with the children and the various programmes. Maybe by the end of the day you'll choose an area you'd like to stay in. I think every teacher could do with another pair of hands."

"Okay," replied Kristy.

She stepped out of the office and into the corridor. Directly opposite her was a doorway. A sign next to it read "Study Hall". Kristy peeped inside. She saw several long tables with chairs, a bookshelf holding a set of encyclopaedias, a cupboard labelled "Supplies", and walls lined with children's pictures and art projects. Several kids were sitting sloppily at the tables, surrounded by open books, lined paper, homework pads, jackets, sweaters, gym bags. . . .

Kristy walked into the room.

The kids perked up.

"Can you help me?" a boy called out immediately.

"Okay," replied Kristy. "I mean—probably. What do you need help with?"

"Spelling."

"Oh, okay. I'm good at that." Kristy glanced round. A teacher was busy with a little girl who was reading aloud, sounding out each word. The teacher nodded to Kristy, and went on working.

Kristy settled herself at a table, opposite the boy.

"My name is Oliver," the boy whispered.

"Hi, I'm Kristy."

"Okay." Oliver smiled. "Do you know how to spell *Leonardo* and *Donatello*?"

Kristy raised her eyebrows. Oliver couldn't have been more than eight. "What are you working on?" asked Kristy. "A report?"

"No, a writing assignment."

"About famous artists?"

Oliver shook his head. "I'm writing about my heroes, the Teenage Mutant Hero Turtles," he whispered.

Kristy succeeded in not laughing. She spelled the words for Oliver, helped another boy with his maths homework, and settled a squabble between two girls over a rubber. Then the teacher stood up.

"Snack time!" she announced. "Anyone who needs a break, go into the kitchen." The room emptied as the children scrambled into the corridor.

Kristy followed them halfway. She

paused at the doorway to the room where the babies were napping in their cots. She walked on. Halfway to the kitchen, she ran into Mrs Hall.

"The three-year-olds need some help," Mrs Hall announced. "Why their teacher chose *today* to finger paint is beyond me."

Kristy headed for the playroom used by the three- and four-year-olds. She opened the door and was greeted by a flustered-looking young man who said to her breathlessly, "I don't know who you are, but who*ever* you are, thank goodness you're here . . . Stephen! The paint goes on the paper, not in your hair. Aimee! Oh, for heaven's . . . Christopher!"

"Have they ever finger painted before?" Kristy wanted to know.

"Yes, but never on a day when they've missed their naps."

"Their *naps*?"

The man nodded. "Both of them. We went on an outing this morning—"

"To the farm, to the *farm*, to the FARM!" sang Aimee, giggling.

Her teacher tried to pull himself together. "Yes, to a farm. And this afternoon, the kids were still keyed up, and naptime came and went and . . . Oh, by the way, I'm Randy Walker."

"I'm Kristy Thomas. What can I do to help you?"

"Supervise that table?" said Randy. He

pointed at the table around which were standing Stephen, Aimee, Christopher, and two other children. "I'll watch the kids at this table. We're going to paint for about ten more minutes, then I think I'll read to the kids and try to calm them down before their parents arrive. Grab yourself a smock."

Kristy noticed that Randy and the children were each wearing a smock, an oversized shirt buttoned down the back. She found an extra, hanging by the sink, and put it on. Then she approached Aimee's table.

"Hey, look!" exclaimed Aimee. "Red and blue and green and yellow and purple make brown."

Her painting was a big muddy blob. (Her hands were the same colour.)

"That's, um, lovely," said Kristy. "Hey, Stephen, how about making designs on *your* paper?"

Stephen was marching spiritedly around the table, making squiggles on everyone else's paintings.

Christopher burst into tears. "You've wrecked it!" he cried.

"Did not!" (Stephen began to cry, too.)

"Whoa, you two," said Kristy. She separated them (glad she was wearing the smock) and began to sing the first song that came to mind, which happened to be "Rock Around the Clock".

Christopher and Stephen stopped crying.

Aimee wrote AIMEE on her brown painting and announced that she had finished.

A few minutes later, the children were putting away the paints and washing their hands at the sink. Randy asked Christopher to choose a story, and he walked to a bookcase and returned with *Ask Mr Bear*.

When the children had settled sleepily on the floor, Kristy tiptoed out of the door. How was she going to decide where to work? So far, she liked the older kids *and* the three-year-olds. She had a feeling she would like the other age groups as well. And she did. She read aloud to some five-year-olds. She helped a group of ten-year-old girls make beaded jewellery. She supervised a group of boys who were playing football in the playground.

She was passing round crackers to the toddlers when Mrs Hall stuck her head in the room. "Kristy?" she said. "I'm sorry to take you away from this, but Miss Preiss needs some help with the little ones."

"Okay," said Kristy.

She followed Mrs Hall into the room where the babies were being fed. She took a quick count—eight babies, two . . . teachers? (What exactly did you call the adults who worked with the infants? Kristy settled for their names, Marcia and Sandy.) Five of the babies were sitting in high chairs, two were reclining in infant seats, and the eighth was being walked around the room by Sandy. He cried loudly. Sandy sang to him and patted his back.

Meanwhile, Marcia was trying to feed the seven remaining babies. Kristy could see why another pair of hands was needed. Without being told, she found some facecloths and sponged off sticky faces and hands.

"Ah-da-da!" cried one little girl. (She was wearing overalls, and had almost no hair, but Kristy could tell she was a girl because of the ruffly pink band that had been placed around her head.) She bounced up and down in the high chair.

"I think Joy has finished," said Marcia. "How are you at changing nappies, Kristy?" Marcia looked pretty uncomfortable. "I hate to ask, but . . ."

"That's okay," Kristy replied. She lifted Joy out of her high chair.

"Everything you need is in the other room." Marcia pointed to a doorway, through which Kristy could see cots and two changing tables.

Kristy carried Joy into the empty room. "Here you go, Miss Joy," she said, settling the baby on one of the tables. "I'm going to clean you up and—"

"Wahhh!" wailed Joy.

"Sorry," called Marcia. "Joy is never thrilled about having her nappy changed."

Kristy sang a couple of verses of "Rock Around the Clock", ignoring Joy's wailing.

When the nappy had been changed, she lifted Joy and danced her around the room. Joy smiled (and drooled). Then abruptly she began to whimper.

"What's the matter?" Kristy asked her. "I wish you could talk." She walked and hummed, and slowly Joy's cries subsided. Kristy sat in a rocking chair, with Joy in her lap. Back and forth they went. Joy's eyes began to close. Kristy watched. And listened. She stopped humming. Joy's breathing became deep and regular and even.

She was sound asleep.

Now what? wondered Kristy. She looked up and saw Marcia standing in the doorway, smiling. "You must have the magic touch," she said. "Joy *never* falls asleep that quickly."

Kristy smiled, flattered. "I'm afraid to put her in a cot, though," she said. "I don't want to wake her up."

So Kristy held Joy until Joy's mother arrived to take her home. Later, when Mrs Hall asked Kristy where she wanted to work the next time she came to the centre, Kristy didn't even hesitate before she answered, "With the babies."

7th
CHAPTER

Back to the Kids Club. My third afternoon at Stoneybrook Elementary started off nicely. "You're doing a great job, Jessi," Mr Katz told me.

I beamed. "Well, I'm having a great time." I was sure that at the end of the next meeting, Mr Katz would ask me to stay on until Miss Simon returned.

The kids entered the room. Some ran. (Nicky ran, leaped up, and tried to touch the door frame over his head, then hurtled on inside.) Some walked. (Becca and Charlotte were among them). Bruce managed to *dance* into the room.

And then a frail little girl peered through the doorway. She was thin (I could tell that, even though she was dressed in an oversized top and oversized jeans), and a bright red scarf covered her head.

Across the front of her T-shirt were the words BALD IS BEAUTIFUL.

She had to be Danielle Roberts.

"Danielle!" exclaimed Mr Katz. "Come on in."

"Mr Katz!" Danielle flung herself into Mr Katz's arms. He pretended to be knocked off balance, and Danielle giggled.

"We are *so* glad you decided to come back to the club," he said warmly.

"And *I* am *so* glad to be back at school."

"No!"

"Yes! Honestly. I'm glad for homework and reports and even maths."

"You hate maths," said Mr Katz.

"Not as much as the hospital."

While Danielle and Mr Katz talked, I observed first Danielle and then the other children in the room.

I had to admit that Danielle didn't look wonderful, although she had probably been quite pretty before she became ill. Her face was small and thin, and her eyes were huge and brown, shaded by long lashes. Her eyes flashed when she spoke. And she smiled a lot.

On the other hand, she was painfully thin. Under her eyes were dark circles. And on her hands and arms were several bruises. Also, even if she hadn't been wearing the T-shirt, anyone would have known she was nearly bald. She couldn't hide that with a

61

kerchief. And I'm sorry to say this, but she looked pretty odd. No matter how prepared you think you are, you don't expect to see an almost-bald nine-year-old girl. She looked like a little old man.

Most of the other Kids Club members had arrived by then. The third-graders, I noticed, were clustered together not far from Danielle and Mr Katz. They didn't greet Danielle or try to talk to her. Well, that's to be expected, I thought. The eight-year-olds weren't in the Kids Club the year before. They probably didn't know Danielle. But the fourth- and fifth-graders knew her all right. So why were *they* clustered in another area of the room staring at Danielle but not talking to her? Then I realized. They were afraid.

Danielle was great, though. She *must* have noticed her friends' reaction to her. It would have been Lard not to. But Danielle approached the older kids and said (flashing her smile), "Hi, everyone. It's really me."

No response, although a few of the third-graders smiled.

"You know, you don't have to worry," Danielle went on. "I'm not contagious. You can't catch cancer."

A few of the kids seemed to relax a little, although still none of them spoke.

"Um, do you want to ask me anything?" said Danielle.

The older kids shuffled their feet and looked out of the windows, into the corridor, down at the floor—anywhere but at Danielle.

Across the room, Charlotte Johanssen raised her hand.

"Yes?" said Danielle. Then she whispered loudly, "I'm not a teacher. You only have to raise your hand for Mr Katz."

The kids laughed.

"Well," began Charlotte, "I was wondering. Do you—do you *still* have cancer? I thought you were getting well in the hospital."

"I was. I mean I am better," replied Danielle. "But the doctors want to make *sure* the cancer has really gone. I still take a lot of medicine."

Danielle sat on a desk and propped her feet on a chair. The third-graders immediately sat on the floor around her. The older kids followed, but more slowly. Why, I wondered, were the fourth-and fifth-graders so stand-offish and afraid—but not the third-graders? Becca and Charlotte were not usually noted for their bravery.

"Danielle?" spoke up Nicky Pike in a small voice. "What's under your scarf?" Nicky was not being cheeky. He wasn't laughing. The other kids were solemn, too.

Danielle grinned. "What's under my scarf?" she repeated. "Not much!"

This got a big laugh from *every*body.

Then the room grew silent and stayed like that for almost a minute. Mr Katz had retreated to his desk and was sitting behind it, allowing the kids to work out things for themselves. So I retreated, too. I took a seat near Mr Katz.

At long last, Vanessa Pike said hesitantly, "Danielle, I hope you aren't offended or anything, but . . . you don't look like yourself. And it isn't just because of your hair. I mean, you're so thin . . ."

Then I understood why the older kids seemed afraid. They were afraid *for* Danielle. She didn't look the way she'd looked at the end of the last school year. The kids were comparing the Danielle who sat in front of them with their memories of a healthy Danielle. The third-graders couldn't do that, since this was the first time they'd met her. To them, she was a curiosity and not much more. To the others, she was a friend who was obviously ill.

"Yeah," said Danielle. "I know I'm thin. It's the chemo."

"What's chemo?" someone asked.

"It means chemotherapy. Fighting cancer with drugs. Only the drugs are really strong, and they make you feel sick a lot. They also made my hair fall out."

"Will your hair grow back?" my sister wanted to know."

"Yup," replied Danielle. "And guess what. It might grow back different. Like, curlier or thicker. That happens sometimes."

"Cool," said Becca.

A fifth-grader spoke up. "If you're still ill, how come you're back at school? I mean, how come you're not in hospital?"

"Because I'm not as ill as I was. I don't need injections all the time. I can take pills. Anyway, I *wanted* to come home. I'd been in hospital a long time. And the hospital is not exactly fun."

"Can you do everything you used to do?" asked a boy.

"Almost," Danielle answered. "I still get tired easily. But my mum says I have to do all my homework. She says cancer isn't an excuse for falling behind."

"Meanie-mo!" exclaimed Vanessa.

After another silence, Bruce asked, "How did you get ill? I mean, you seemed okay at the end of the third grade."

"I was. I felt fine. But over the summer I started getting all these sore throats and temperatures. And I was tired all the time. My parents took me to the doctor and he did a blood test and that was when they found out it wasn't just the flu or something. It was leukaemia."

"Danielle, are you afraid?" asked my sister.

"Sometimes. But I made up a rule as soon as I got home from hospital. The rule is that I will only be ill when I'm *in* hospital. When I'm at home, I'll try to be like everyone else. That means not thinking and worrying about the leukaemia all the time. I say to myself, 'You are very strong. You are stronger than the leukaemia. You *will* get better.' "

I glanced at Mr Katz, who was smiling, but whose eyes looked awfully bright. I wasn't surprised. I was blinking back tears myself.

A few minutes later, when the kids seemed to have run out of questions, Mr Katz said, "Okay. Are you ready to write to your pen pals?"

The room exploded with activity. The kids *jumped* to their feet. (I think they were all pretty tense.) Danielle was left sitting on the desk, so I approached her. "Hi," I said. "I'm Jessi Ramsey. I'm Becca's sister." I pointed out Becca and Charlotte, who were working across the room. "I'm helping Mr Katz until Miss Simon can come back."

I explained what we were doing and asked Danielle if she wanted to work with a partner.

"No," she replied. (The kids had scattered.) "That's okay. Besides, there are *twelve* kids to write to now. When I left the hospital, two new kids were coming. One is a boy who has leukaemia like me. He's six. I want to write to him."

I helped Danielle work on her letter, even though she didn't seem to need much help. She wanted to talk, though. "You know what my dad says to my little brother and me each night before we go to sleep?" said Danielle. "He says, 'Wish on the North Star.' That's the bright star in the sky. I never tell him, but I always make *two* wishes on the star. I wish that my family and I could go to Disney World. We've never been there. And I wish to graduate from fifth grade and go to middle school."

When the club meeting was over, the kids ran noisily out of the room. Except for Danielle, whose mother picked her up. Danielle was tired and droopy. As they walked down the corridor, I made a wish of my own. I wished that Danielle would recover.

8th CHAPTER

The barn was hot and dusty—and peaceful. I lay against a bale of hay and breathed in the barn smells. I watched the sun shine through a small window high above me. "You two are so lucky," I said to Dawn and Mary Anne. "How come you don't *live* in the barn?"

Dawn grinned. "Too hot in the summer, too cold in the winter."

"Oh. Well, you're lucky anyway."

The house that Dawn's mum bought is a colonial farmhouse. Behind it stands an immense old barn. Dawn and Mary Anne and their parents don't use it for anything much, except storage. It's a great place to hold club meetings, though. Except that there's no phone. And no electricity. And no hidden junk food . . . Okay, so it isn't perfect. But it's a nice change.

On a Saturday afternoon, the members of

68

the BSC arrived at the barn for a meeting. An unofficial one. The seven of us hadn't been in the same place at the same time for ages. (Well, for about two weeks.) And we missed each other.

Now we were going to get together to discuss our new projects.

"Hello?" called someone from below us.

"Come on up. We're in the hayloft!" Mary Anne replied.

Several seconds later, Stacey's head appeared at the top of the ladder. She was the last to arrive. She climbed into the loft and stretched out flat on her back. (She was dressed in her grubby clothes.) "This is the life," she said with a sigh. "I think I was meant to be a country girl."

"You mean, life without Bloomingdale's?" asked Claud.

"Oh. No. What was I thinking? I'm not a country girl at all. My mistake."

Claud laughed. So did Kristy.

Then Kristy said, "Okay, everyone. As you know, this isn't an official meeting of the Babysitters Club."

"Right. No phone, no alarm clock, no visor," said Mallory.

"We're just here to talk." Kristy was smiling. "So. What's new?"

"My job", spoke up Stacey, "is so cool." She paused. "It isn't easy, though."

"Is something wrong?" I asked.

"Not really. No," said Stace. "I was prepared for problems, I suppose. The thing is the boy, Gordon, is great. He asks lots of questions, and he follows my advice. But Charmaine will *not* listen to me. She's trying to pretend she isn't ill. She gets her insulin because her parents give her the injections. But she doesn't stick to her diet. She says that turning down sweets reminds her she has a disease. So she eats them. But, of course, then she doesn't feel well. I think she's really frustrated. Which I can understand."

"Have you told her that?" asked Mary Anne.

"What? That I think she's frustrated?" replied Stace.

"No, that you *understand* that she's frustrated. She'd probably like to know that. Tell her how hard it is for you to stick to your diet."

"Hey, that's a good idea!" exclaimed Stacey. "I've been trying to be this role model, this perfect person."

"Beep," said Claud. "Wrong. Bad move. Who wants to have to live up to someone perfect? That's much too hard. I used to think I had to be like Janine, which was impossible. Now I know better."

"Well, I'm in *love* with Frankie," said Mary Anne. "What a great little boy. I don't know *why* I'm in love with him, since he can't walk or talk and I never know what's going on in his mind. But he has this incredible smile. And sometimes he'll grin right in the middle of one of his toughest exercises. It's as if he's saying, 'This hurts, but I know you're doing it to help me, so thank you.' "

"I'm in love, too," said Kristy. "With babies."

"Lucky duck," said Mal.

"Yeah. Babies are *so sweet*."

"Gag, gag," said Dawn.

"No, really. And they change so fast. It's hard to believe, when you're holding an infant, that a year later, she'll probably be walking and beginning to talk. She'll be a *person*."

"Danielle is a person," I said quietly.

Six pairs of eyes turned towards me.

"What?" said Claud.

"I said that Danielle is a person. But some people seem to have forgotten that. To almost everyone, especially the other kids, Danielle isn't just a person. She's a kid with cancer. Which is the last thing she wants to be. And I don't mean that Danielle wishes she didn't have leukaemia. She's accepted that she has it. But she wishes people wouldn't treat her so differently. She's still *Danielle*.

"You know what she *does* wish?" I went on.

"No," said Mary Anne. The others shook their heads.

"She has two wishes," I told them. "To take a trip to Disney World with her family. And to graduate from elementary school. Can you believe it? Most kids are thinking, 'When I grow up . . .' or, 'When I'm sixteen . . .' But Danielle isn't looking much beyond the fifth grade right now."

"One of her wishes is to graduate from Stoneybrook Elementary?" repeated Mary Anne. She immediately began to cry.

Everyone else looked pretty tearful, too. Even Kristy.

"Danielle sounds like a great kid," said Claud, in a choked-up voice.

"Oh, she is," I agreed. "I hope you get to meet her some time. You'd love her. She has the *best* sense of humour." I told my friends some of the things Danielle had said when she was talking to the members of the Kids Club. "And she wears a T-shirt that says 'bald is beautiful', " I added.

The tears turned to laughter. (Well, to chuckles.)

"Is there any chance Danielle's first wish will come true?" asked Mary Anne.

"To go to Disney World? I don't know," I replied. "I've met Danielle's mother and we've talked a little. I don't think the Robertses are poor or anything, but I know that Danielle's medical expenses are huge.

Insurance covers some things, but not everything. I don't think they have much extra money now. Not enough to send four people to Disney World."

Mary Anne had stopped crying by this time. "Have you ever heard of something called Your Wish Is My Command?" she wanted to know.

I shook my head. Most of the others looked puzzled, too.

"It's this organization in Stamford," said Mary Anne. "It grants the wishes of children who are ill—kids who've been ill for a long time or who are ill most of the time. Especially kids whose illnesses have been expensive for their families. Kids like Danielle."

"What kinds of wishes?" asked Mallory.

"Almost any kind," Mary Anne replied. "Little kids sometimes just want toys their parents can't afford. Older kids usually want to go to Disney World or Disneyland. Sometimes they want to get together with relatives they haven't seen for a long time. Some kids want to meet stars. YWIMC grants as many wishes as they can. They get the money from donations."

"Cool!" I exclaimed. "Boy, if Danielle could go to Disney World, she . . . I mean, her family . . . I don't know. I just think a trip like that would be great for the Robertses. They *all* need a holiday. They've practically lived in that hospital recently. I bet they can hardly think of anything except medicine and treatments and leukaemia and money. And Danielle has a great attitude, but she *is* just a kid. I'm sure she'd like to spend a few days in a place where she isn't Danielle Roberts, the girl with cancer. Even Mr Katz, who is so wonderful, sometimes overprotects Danielle. It's hard not to. But if Mr Katz overprotects her, think what her parents must do, even if they try to treat her just the way they used to."

My friends and I talked until the sky clouded over and the barn grew cool.

"The meeting might as well be adjourned," said Kristy then. "Remember—anyone who's free, go to Claud's on Monday at five-thirty to answer the phone."

We left the barn then, and I went home on my bicycle, pedalling fast to beat the rain. I just made it. As I was putting my bike in our garage, I heard a clap of thunder. Ordinarily, I quite like storms, but I couldn't think about this one. My mind was so busy with wishes.

I found the phone book in our kitchen, turned to the Stamford pages, and looked up Your Wish Is My Command. Would anyone answer the phone on a Saturday? Probably not.

"Hello? Your Wish Is My Command."

A volunteer had picked up the phone. I asked him a zillion questions about the organization. Who could have a wish granted? How long would it take? What process did the family have to go through? Then I told him about Danielle and her wishes. The man was really nice. He answered my questions patiently. He listened to what I had to say. And *then* he said, "Ask Danielle's mother or father to give us a call."

It was as simple as that.

I said thank you and hung up. I turned to the Stoneybrook section of the phone book. A lot of families are named Roberts, but I picked out Danielle's family easily. Her parents are named Ray and Faye!

I dialled the number.

Mrs Roberts answered.

"Hi," I said. "This is Jessi Ramsey from the Kids Club. Um, Mrs Roberts, I've just found out the most wonderful thing. . . ."

9th CHAPTER

Tuesday

Give me a hart atack! This afternon was fun but wild. I helped out at the art class and the kids were making clay scluptures. They are even going to be glased and fied fired. A profeshional projeck. I would have never thought of leting 7-year olds do a projeck like this but they are having a grate time and they're not all making plain dishes ether. Some of them are working on pretty good scluptures. If only there was some way they cold get rid of there energy befor art class started.

Kristy's stepsister Karen is so much like Kristy that it's weird. She and Kristy didn't know each other until shortly before Karen's dad married Kristy's mum, but they could be twins. Not in terms of looks. Karen has wide blue eyes, long blonde hair, and freckles, and she wears glasses. She and Kristy are not even remotely similar. Unless you get to know them. Karen is as full of ideas as Kristy is. She has just as much energy, if not more. And she is a talker. Also, she tends to get noisy. Adults always have to remind her to use her "indoor voice".

So try to imagine Karen in Claudia's art class at the community centre. Of course, Claud and the other teacher were in charge of not just Karen but eleven other seven-year-olds, including Margo Pike and Jackie Rodowsky. The members of the BSC adore Jackie, but we refer to him as "the walking disaster", because of his constant accidents—tripping, falling, spilling, breaking, you name it. He doesn't do those things on purpose. But if there's so much as a bit of fluff on the carpet, you can bet Jackie will stumble over it.

All right. *Now* imagine these kids making sculptures out of clay, glazing them, and firing them in a kiln. This is what Claudia meant by a professional project. The kids weren't making plasticine creations that would never dry. Or even clay pieces that would dry into a chalky grey mess. *Their* sculptures would look shiny and ceramic. Actual pottery.

The art teacher, Mr Renfrew, had told the kids they could make whatever they wanted. Claudia walked from pupil to pupil, answering questions and helping. The kids were seated at long tables that formed a square. The classroom was small and crowded—but Claud didn't mind. She had a feeling that open space would have encouraged running around.

"Can you tell what I'm making?" Margo Pike asked as Claud paused next to her, peering at the wet clay that oozed between Margo's fingers.

Claud considered the brown blob. It didn't look like much of anything. And she didn't want to hurt Margo's feelings by making the wrong guess. Luckily (or un-luckily; it was hard to say), before she had a chance to answer, she heard someone say, "Uh-oh."

It was Jackie. Claud knew that without even looking round.

"What's happened?" she asked.

"Nothing," said Jackie, which in Jackie-talk means, "Something."

"Hey!" How come there's clay all over the floor?" exclaimed Karen Brewer.

"I was *try*ing", said Jackie, "to make a snake. And I was squeezing the clay and it shot out of my hands."

"It flew right past me," Karen started to say indignantly. Then she stopped talking and stared at the clay that had come to rest on the floor. "A snake! Oh, that's a good idea!" she cried. "Jungles need snakes." Karen forgot about Jackie and returned to her sculpture.

Claud glanced at Mr Renfrew, who was busy across the room, and then at Jackie, who was holding out his hands helplessly.

"This stuff's slimy," he complained. "Hey, just like snakes!"

"Snakes are not slimy," Karen informed him. "They have scales."

"So do fish, and fish are slimy," replied Jackie.

"Okay, you two," said Claud. "Karen, work on your jungle, please. Jackie, help me clean up your clay, please."

"Why does clay have to be so gloopy?" asked Jackie. He was on his hands and knees, retrieving the clay. He looked like someone trying to pick up a wet bar of soap. (Claud hid a smile.)

"The clay is wet", she said to Jackie, "so you can mould it more easily."

"Oh." Jackie settled down.

"*Now* guess what I'm making!" cried Margo.

Claudia winced. Then she took another look at Margo's clay—which had changed from a blob to . . .

"A person!" said Claudia. "It's a statue of a person."

"Yup." Margo nodded. "A whole person. Head, body, arms, legs."

The boy next to Margo glanced at her work. "It looks like a hamburger," he said.

"Reid!" cried Karen. "That is not nice. You've made Margo feel bad. Now she's going to cry, aren't you, Margo?"

"Yes," Margo answered, even though she had looked fine. Her lower lip began to tremble, followed by her chin.

"But it *does* look like a hamburger," said Reid.

"It's a Hamburger Man!" added Jackie.

Margo bit her lip. Then she started to smile. "Yeah! It's a Hamburger Man!" she exclaimed. "I'll give him lettuce and tomato for a hat, and . . ."

"How's your jungle?" Claud asked Karen.

"Well, elephants are hard to make. Did I do his ears right?"

The ears, in fact, looked awful, but Claudia answered the question by saying, "I could tell straight away that it was an elephant."

"You could? Goody. And this is going to be a purple tree—"

"A purple tree?" interrupted Reid.

"Yes, a purple tree," Karen answered defensively. "And now, right here, sliming along on the floor of the jungle is," (Karen paused dramatically) "a blue snake."

"I thought you said snakes aren't slimy," said Jackie. He had finished cleaning up his mess and was energetically rolling his clay into a lengthy snake.

"I did," Karen replied. "And I did *not* say my snake was slimy. I said he was sliming along. I can say that if I want."

"Why's your snake going to be blue?" Reid asked Karen. "Snakes are green."

"Not all of them. Besides, if I made my snake green and my tree green, then almost my whole jungle would be—" Karen stopped speaking suddenly. She stared, entranced, at her creation.

Margo glanced up. "Karen?" she said questioningly.

Karen didn't answer. But her eyes slowly grew wide and round. She looked like an owl. Or like a cat about to pounce.

"What's going on?" Claudia asked warily.

Karen spoke in a whisper. "Look at the elephant. His trunk is moving."

Six kids jumped up and crowded around Karen.

"Ahem," said Mr Renfrew.

The kids took their seats again.

But Karen continued to stare at her nearly completed sculpture. And the children continued to stare at Karen.

"Don't you see it?" said Karen hoarsely, not taking her eyes off the elephant.

Claudia said it was at this point that Karen began to give her the creeps.

Jackie Rodowsky remained seated, but leaned over to peer at the elephant. Suddenly he cried, "Oh! The elephant's trunk *is* moving! I think."

"The whole jungle is alive!" Karen exclaimed softly. "The branches of the tree are swaying, the snake is sliming, and now . . . yes, now the elephant is walking. He's walking towards the snake."

"Aaaghhh! He's going to *step* on the snake!" cried Reid. "Then you'll really have slime. Stop the elephant, Karen!"

Well, of course, *nothing* was moving on Karen's sculpture. The kids were suffering from a massive dose of overactive imaginations. Still, Claudia knew she had to get everyone under control. She didn't want Mr Renfrew to think she wasn't doing her job. "Karen?" she said.

"What?" (Karen's eyes were glued to her jungle.)

"It's a shame about your sculpture. I'm really sorry."

Karen finally moved. She raised her eyes to meet Claud's. "What do you mean?"

"We've got to glaze the sculptures and get ready to fire them in the kiln. But we can't do either thing to your jungle." Claudia looked terribly sad and apologetic.

"Why can't we?" Karen wanted to know.

"Are you kidding? Put a live tree and a live elephant and a live snake in an oven and *fire* them?"

"Oh. I suppose we *can't* do that." Karen regarded the sculpture again. Then she leaned over and stared at it intently. Finally she said, "You know, I think everything has stopped moving. . . . Yup. I just see a clay elephant and a clay tree and a clay snake. How could clay move?"

"But Karen," began Margo, "I thought you—"

"Okay, my jungle is all finished," Karen interrupted. "Time to glaze it and burn it. I mean, cook it. I mean, um—"

"Fire it," supplied Claudia.

"Yeah, fire it."

Claud breathed a sigh of relief. Around her, the kids were returning to rolling and moulding and flattening and poking their lumps of clay. The Hamburger Man now wore a lettuce-and-tomato hat. Margo was busily making bacon strips (which looked a lot like flattened snakes).

What would happen during the glazing and firing of the sculptures, Claud could only imagine. But she thought she could handle anything.

10th CHAPTER

"She isn't really weird," Becca said.

"I never said she was, did I?" I replied.

"No. But some of the other kids think so."

Becca was talking about Danielle. She was sitting cross-legged at the end of my bed, dangerously close to the edge. She looked so serious that I didn't even bother to tell her to watch out. I didn't want to interrupt her thoughts.

"How do you know?" I asked.

Becca gazed past me, out of the window into the night. "They talk about her," she said after a while. "They talk behind her back. Sometimes they forget and talk to *me*. Or to Charlotte."

Which was pretty thoughtless, considering that Becca and Charlotte had become friends with Danielle. The three of them didn't see much of each other during school, since Danielle is in the fourth grade, and Charlotte and my sister are in the third, but they had become nearly inseparable during meetings of the Kids Club. They had cooked up several good ideas together. And the three of them were champion gigglers.

"I don't understand it," Becca said to me that night. "It's like, after you get to know Danielle, you don't even think about her bald head or her medicine. You forget she has cancer. *You* don't think about diabetes every time you see Stacey, do you?" (I shook my head. No.) "But the other kids won't even try to get to know Danielle—and most of them knew her last year! They act as if she's from another planet. Well, not all of them. But a lot of them. "Becca paused thoughtfully. Then she went on, "At least they don't say unkind things *to* her. That would be awful."

"Why do you think the kids protect her like that?" I asked. "I mean, why do they go to the trouble of talking *behind* her back?"

"I don't know. I suppose they don't want to hurt her feelings."

"That's a start, isn't it?" I said.

"I suppose so." Becca smiled at me.

The next day, Becca asked Mama if Danielle could come over to play on Saturday. "Charlotte, too," added Becca.

"I don't see why not," said Mama, "if it's okay with Danielle's parents."

It was.

So at eleven o'clock on Saturday morning, Mrs Roberts dropped off Danielle at our house. She and Mama talked for a few minutes. Then Mrs Roberts kissed Danielle, said, "Remember your medicine," and, "I'll be back at about four," and drove off.

Becca and Danielle looked at each other joyously. What a pair they made—Becca, dark-skinned, shorter and chunkier than Danielle, wearing a new pair of dungarees, her thick hair put in ponytails; and Danielle, still pale, with the shape of a bean pole, wearing droopy jeans and her even droopier BALD IS BEAUTIFUL T-shirt, a blue-and-green scarf not really hiding her almost bald head.

I don't think either one of them noticed, though. Besides, they didn't have time to stand around thinking about themselves. They had plans—and plenty of them—for the day.

"First we phone Charlotte," said Becca, heading for the phone.

"Jessi?" said Mama. "Can you keep an eye on the girls and Squirt for a while? Daddy and I want to work in the garden. Aunt Cecelia's out for the day."

"Of course," I replied.

86

"The garden" is a rose bed that my parents planted in our back garden. It's their pride and joy. They work on it every weekend that they can.

Mama and Daddy left through the garage door.

Becca hung up the phone and announced to anyone in earshot that Charlotte was on her way. "And she's bringing her Barbies."

"Uh-oh," said Danielle. "I've left my Barbies at home."

"That's okay. I have twelve. You can borrow a few," Becca said generously.

Charlotte turned up, Barbie case in tow. I knew perfectly well what was inside that case: three battered Barbie dolls, a jumble of clothing, a reel of cotton, a yo-yo missing its string, and a small torch. (When asked what the cotton, the yo-yo, and the torch were for, Charlotte merely shrugged and said, "It's stuff I need.")

"Hi!" cried Becca as she let Char inside. "Here's Danielle. She forgot her Barbies, but she's going to borrow some of mine."

"Okay," said Char. "Hey, Becca, why don't you lend five to Danielle and two to me? That way, we can each have five."

This seemed to be an important point. Once Becca had agreed to it, the girls charged upstairs. I turned to Squirt, who was sitting on the floor. He had been watching the girls, probably wishing he was old enough to be a part of things. He grinned at me.

"How about a piggy-back ride?" I said. I settled Squirt on my back and ran him around the house. We were passing the staircase when I heard shrieking upstairs. So I backed up and then ran to the first floor.

"What's going on?" I called.

The shrieking stopped.

"Nothing," Becca finally called back.

I skidded to a halt at the doorway to Becca's room.

"Moy!" cried Squirt.

"No more," I told him. "Not now. Becca—?"

"We're not hurt," Becca assured me, before I could say a word about the red streaks that crisscrossed her face, as well as Char's and Danielle's.

"It's our war paint," added Charlotte.

"We're Red Indian warriors," Danielle informed me.

"What happened to playing Barbie?" I asked.

The girls looked at each other guiltily. They removed their Barbies from various carrying cases. Each Barbie was wearing her own war paint.

When the girls and the dolls had been cleaned up, I led the girls downstairs.

"Okay," said Danielle. "It's time for . . . Squirt Tag!"

Nobody, not even Danielle, knew what Squirt Tag was. Nevertheless, a noisy, energetic chase ensued. The girls followed Squirt around the house. Squirt ran just ahead of them, giggling. The girls pretended that Squirt could move faster than they could. They pretended to be unable to catch him. When Squirt tripped and fell down, the girls fell down, too.

"Okay, everybody outside!" I said as the kids got to their feet.

"Outside for a game of The Return of Squirt Tag!" shouted Danielle.

The kids ran around the back garden. When they started to look sweaty, I called, "Who wants lemonade?"

"Me!" cried the girls. (Squirt put up his hand.)

I picked up my little brother. Becca and Charlotte dashed for the house. Danielle lagged behind them. As I held the door open for her, I thought she looked paler than usual, which seemed odd, because Char and my sister and Squirt were flushed from all the running around.

Danielle walked inside, completely out of breath. She headed for the nearest sofa and collapsed onto it. Then she lay sprawled on her back, her eyes closed. She barely moved.

"Danielle?" whispered Becca. (She looked scared to death.)

"I can't move," Danielle murmured.

I put Squirt on the floor and ran to Danielle. "What's wrong?" I cried.

Danielle opened her eyes. "Oh, don't worry. I'm okay."

"You don't look okay."

"But I am. Honest." Danielle struggled to sit up. "I shouldn't have run around so much. That's all."

"Well, have you got a temperature or what?"

"A temperature? No, I just got too tired. I need to rest for a while."

"All right," I replied. My mind was racing. "Charlotte, why don't you get Danielle a glass of water? Becca, you keep Danielle company. I'll be right back."

I picked up Squirt again and ran to my parents in the garden. I told them what had happened. They dashed inside, took a look at Danielle, who already seemed better, and decided to call her parents anyway. But no one answered the phone.

"I really, really am fine," Danielle assured us.

Since she did, in fact, look better, Mama and Daddy relaxed a little.

Danielle sat up. Some colour had returned to her cheeks. "Let's play Barbies again," she said to Becca. So Becca brought the dolls, their clothes, and all their accessories into the living room. She and Danielle and Charlotte played together until four o'clock. But Danielle never left the sofa.

"I shouldn't have played so hard this morning," she said. "But sometimes I forget that I can't play the way I used to. Oh, well. I'll learn."

Mr and Mrs Roberts arrived at our house at exactly 3:55 that afternoon. I told Mrs Roberts that Danielle had got overtired. I felt I had to.

"She *does* get overtired," Mrs Roberts agreed, "but she knows how to deal with that. I'm sorry we weren't at home when you called, though. We—Oh! I can't believe I didn't tell you this right away. Someone from YWIMC called this afternoon. He said Danielle has been placed on their 'wish list'. That means that as soon as enough money is donated, Danielle's wish can be granted."

"All right!" I exclaimed. With a little luck, Danielle might get to go to Disney World after all.

11th CHAPTER

One evening, Becca and I had a nice surprise. The surprise was a phone call from Danielle.

"Guess what!" she cried.

I almost said, "Has your wish been granted? Are you going to Disney World?" Luckily, I didn't say that. First of all, I remembered, just in time, that Danielle didn't know about YWIMC. If her wish was granted, it was going to be a surprise for her. Second, what if that wasn't the news anyway? So I caught myself and simply said, "What?"

"Mummy and Daddy are going to have a barbecue on Saturday night, and they said that you and Becca and Charlotte are invited!"

"Fantastic!"

"Charlotte's already said she can come. Can you and Becca come, too?"

"I think so. I'll have to check."

"I *hope* you can. Because we're going to barbecue chicken and hamburgers and hot dogs. And Daddy is going to make his special potato salad. And Mummy and I are going to make brownies, or maybe a cake. Oh, and Greg is going to mix up the lemonade." (Greg is Danielle's brother. He's six and a half.)

"It sounds like a lot of fun," I said. "Becca or I will call you back."

It turned out that Becca and I were both free, so late on Saturday afternoon Charlotte Johanssen came round, and Daddy drove her and Becca and me to Danielle's house. Becca and Charlotte had been there before. I hadn't.

Daddy pulled up in front of a small brick house. The lawn in front was sort of scraggy (if you know what I mean), but someone obviously tended the two flower beds very carefully.

"There's Danielle!" cried Becca, as she opened the door. "See you later, Daddy!"

"Thank you for the lift, Mr Ramsey," added Charlotte politely.

Becca was already running across the lawn. "Oh, good! You're wearing the T-shirt!" she said to Danielle. (For some reason, Becca just loved that BALD IS BEAUTIFUL shirt. She was ecstatic each time Danielle wore it.)

"Hi, girls!" Mrs Roberts called from the front door. "Danielle, slow down."

Danielle leaned conspiratorially towards Becca and Charlotte. "I had a headache earlier today," she whispered. "Mummy made me rest all afternoon. I got *so* bored. I'm really glad you're here."

"Do you have to rest during the barbecue?" asked Charlotte.

"I hope not," Danielle replied. "Come on inside, you two. Hey, Jessi, you haven't met Mr Toes yet."

"Who's Mr Toes?" I asked.

"Our new kitten. Well, really he's Greg's new kitten, but he seems to belong to everyone in the family."

Becca, Charlotte and I followed Danielle inside—and right through her house and out of the back door.

"Mr Toes is so sweet," Becca informed me on the way. "He's all grey except for his toes, which are white. That's why Greg named him Mr Toes."

On the back patio were Mr Roberts and Greg. Mr Roberts was wearing an apron and a chef's hat. He was standing over the barbecue, flipping hamburgers and turning pieces of chicken. Greg was on his hands and knees, peering inside a grocery bag that was lying on its side.

"Mr Toooooes, Mr Tooooooes," he was calling softly.

A grey bundle of fur darted out of the bag, then back inside.

"Well," said Danielle, "that was Mr Toes. He moves fast."

We played with Mr Toes until dinner was ready. Danielle's mother had laid the picnic table with a red-and-white-checked cloth, paper plates, and plastic forks and knives.

"This looks fantastic," I said, as Mr Roberts put down a bowl of potato salad.

Danielle's parents did everything they could to make the picnic special. When supper was over, we roasted marshmallows on the barbecue. Then we sang songs. Mr Roberts even sent Becca, Charlotte, Danielle, and Greg on a treasure hunt. (The prize was a book of jokes.) While the kids followed the clues, which led them round the back garden, I sat with Mr and Mrs Roberts. I watched them as they watched the kids. Mostly, they smiled. The kids were clowning around. Danielle kept shouting, "X marks the spot! X marks the spot!" and Greg rushed after her, crying, "Buried treasure!" and, "Yo ho ho! We are pirates!"

But sometimes this very thoughtful expression would come over the Roberts's faces. I thought I knew why. Four energetic children were tearing around the garden. There was Greg, with his sturdy legs and his shock of reddish-brown hair. There was Becca, who seemed to have endless energy and was always the one sent up trees or behind bushes to search for clues. There was Charlotte, her long, dark hair pulled into a fat plait, dashing after Becca. And there was Danielle, with her knobbly knees and elbows, her slightly askew scarf that showed her bald head quite plainly, and her BALD IS BEAUTIFUL shirt.

What did her parents think as they watched her? Did they remember barbecues from a year earlier, when Danielle was strong and healthy and had hair like her brother's? Did they wonder whether they would have another barbecue, just like this one, a year from then? Did they hope? Did they try *not* to hope? Did they try to forget?

"Danielle!" called Mrs Roberts, standing up. "Pill time!"

"Right *now*?" exclaimed Greg. "Right in the middle of our treasure hunt?"

"Yes, right now," said Mrs Roberts. "Danielle, come on, darling."

"Is Danielle going to get a piece of chocolate after she takes her pills?" asked Greg. "Because if she is, that's not fair. I mean, if she is, I want a piece of chocolate, too. I want—"

"Greg, you don't have to take pills," said Mr Roberts.

"And Danielle, you do. Come here, please."

Danielle trotted across the grass to her mother.

Mrs Roberts rested her hand on Danielle's forehead. "Feeling okay?"

Danielle nodded. "I'm fine. I want to finish the treasure hunt."

"Okay. After your pills. And when the treasure hunt is over, Becca and Jessi and Charlotte will have to go home. You need to go to bed."

"All right."

"But *I'm* not tired," whined Greg. "I don't want everyone to go home. I want to stay up and play. I want . . ." Greg trailed off. He watched his sister follow Mrs Roberts into the house.

Then he sighed.

I decided that having a brother or sister who's sick must be awfully difficult. Greg probably didn't understand much about leukaemia—except that because of it, his sister had spent a lot of time in hospital. So had his parents, too. And that Greg spent a lot of time with neighbours and his grandparents. And that after Danielle came home, people gave *her* most of the attention. I wasn't too surprised when, a little later, Greg flung himself on the ground and threw a tantrum, yelling, "I wish I was ill, too!" (Mr and Mrs Roberts tried to ignore him.)

By the time Daddy arrived to take Becca and Charlotte and me home, Greg was quiet. And Becca had run out of steam. It was only nine o'clock, but she'd been pretty active. Charlotte was tired, too. Danielle was nearly asleep.

The girls called exhausted goodbyes to each other, and then we left. That night, I couldn't stop thinking about Danielle and her family. They needed a holiday badly, I thought. I hoped that Danielle's wish would come true soon.

Guess what happened the next afternoon. My friends and I decided to hold another weekend BSC meeting. But this time the meeting was held in my room! That was a first. I felt honoured.

However, I decided my room didn't look fit for a meeting. So I spent two hours cleaning it. I swept dustballs out from under my bed. Those dustballs must have been as old as I was. Well, not really. But they had probably started forming the day we moved into the house. I dusted my collection of ceramic horses. I wiped the glass covering my ballet posters. I straightened up my stuffed animals, and I organized my books.

I finished just as our doorbell rang. A few moments later, Mary Anne and Dawn ran upstairs. Soon we were joined by Kristy, Mallory, Claud, and Stace.

"Welcome", said Kristy, "to another totally casual BSC meeting. Today's topic of conversation is . . . Our Activities, An Update. I'll start."

Kristy talked about the babies. She especially liked Joy. (Maybe that was because Joy especially liked Kristy.)

"Frankie is making progress," reported Mary Anne. "Just a little, but it's progress anyway. His parents chart his skills so they can actually *see* if he improves. It's sort of hard to tell, if you just watch Frankie. But when you look at the charts and you see that this week Frankie sat up for eight seconds straight, and last week his record was six seconds, then you know you're making a difference. Frankie might be able to crawl one day. Maybe even walk."

"I had a talk with Charmaine," Stacey announced. "I told her that I haven't always been such a great diabetes patient. And I told her about the time when I gorged on chocolate and stuff and finally ended up in hospital. I think I made an impression. Charmaine asked about a zillion questions."

"That's great," said Mal. "I'm having fun at the playground. All the kids are great, but there's this one boy, Danny. He's five years old. I just love him. I know we shouldn't have favourites, and I really try not to. But Danny is so sweet. Yesterday he picked a bouquet of weeds for me."

"I suppose I've sort of singled out Danielle," I said. "I've got to know her family, and . . . and, oh! She might get her wish! She's on the YWIMC wish list!"

"Cool," said Dawn. "I tried not to have favourites, either. But at the Institute I always see a little girl named Kendra. She has cerebral palsy. Boy, you lot should hear about what happens at Baker. . . ."

12th CHAPTER

Monday

I spent another afternoon at the Baker Institute. Kendra was writing a story. She'll be an author one day, I'm sure of that. She is so bright. And she's funny. And when she writes, her words tumble onto the page, sounding just the way she talks, which is helpful for a writer. I can imagine Kendra as an author. She'll go on speaking tours and she'll get interviewed on the radio and maybe on TV, and she'll become famous, and everywhere, people will be talking about the latest book by Kendra Bogdanoff.

Dawn's afternoons at the Baker Institute for physically disabled kids sounded fascinating. She went to Stamford in a specially equipped van with four children from Stoneybrook who went to Baker for physiotherapy, classes in the arts, and a chance to make new friends. The bus driver was a woman who was going to college to learn to be a physiotherapist. She drove the bus to earn some extra money, but the kids were more than just a job to her. She really enjoyed being with them.

"Candace is so *funny*," Dawn told me. "She jokes around with the kids, and they love her. She treats all of them the way you'd treat kids who *aren't* in wheelchairs or wearing leg braces. She'll say to them, 'Hurry up! I haven't got all day', and the kids just giggle. Most people tiptoe round the kids like they're going to break. And never mention their braces or anything. But if a friend of yours got new clothes, you'd make a comment, right? So if a kid gets on the bus with decorations all over the back of his wheelchair, Candace will say, 'Your chair looks great today! I think you should go into business as a decorator.' "

Anyway, when the bus arrived at Baker, Dawn and Candace would help the kids inside. The kids and teachers and therapists would gather in this one huge room and talk. Dawn usually looked around for Kendra. Or Kendra found Dawn.

"Dawn! Yo, Dawn!" Kendra called one afternoon.

Dawn started laughing. She turned round and saw Kendra zipping towards her in her motorized wheelchair.

"What's this 'Yo, Dawn'?" Dawn teased. "What ever happened to 'Good afternoon, Dawn. Nice to see you'?"

"My big brother says 'yo' all the time," replied Kendra. "He even answers the phone that way. He picks it up and he says, 'Yo, the Bogdanoffs'. Who's this?'"

"And what do your parents think of that?" asked Dawn.

"They don't know he does it." Kendra grinned.

Kendra is nine years old. She has cerebral palsy. Her muscles don't work the way most people's muscles do. Her legs don't support her, so she can't stand or walk. And she doesn't have much control over her arms. That's why her wheelchair is motorized. She can steer it just by moving these buttons. She doesn't have to push the wheels along.

When Dawn told me that, I said, "If she doesn't have good muscle control, how can she do *any*thing? You need muscles to write . . . even to see."

"Well, she has better control over some of her muscles than others," Dawn replied. "Also, she uses a computer. It's much easier for her just to hit keys than it is for her to write. Although she *can* write. She can see, too, but she really has to concentrate in order to read. Even so, she reads a lot, which only goes to show how much she enjoys it."

Kendra was always writing something. She really did plan to be an author one day. She was good at writing, and she was proud of her work.

"Look what I wrote last night," Kendra said to Dawn. Slowly she reached into the bag that hung from the side of her chair. She pulled out a piece of paper and held it out towards Dawn.

Dawn reached for it. " 'Why I Hate Tomatoes', " she read aloud. She laughed. "Was this a school assignment?"

"No. My mum made me eat a tomato last night, even though I hate them."

"So you decided to write about that?"

"Yup. My favourite part of my story— well, I suppose it's really more of an essay— is the time I bit into one of those little cherry tomatoes." (Dawn nodded.) "And I squished it between my teeth and the seeds shot all the way across the table and hit my mother in the face. I thought she would say, 'Okay, Kendra. No more tomatoes.' But she didn't. One day I think I'll write a book about tomatoes. I'll call it *My War Against Tomatoes, the Most Disgusting Food There Is*. . . . Hey, there's Polly. Yo, Polly! Wait for me!"

I couldn't help thinking, when Dawn told

me the story, that Kendra was actually luckier than Danielle. I knew I shouldn't compare the girls. I knew there was no point in it. But I couldn't help it. I'm sure both Danielle and Kendra would have thought I was crazy. I mean, take Danielle. Her muscles work fine. She can walk and run and chase after Mr Toes. She doesn't have to concentrate extra hard to read. If she wants to write a quick note, she picks up a pencil and a piece of paper. If she wants to make a phone call, she picks up the phone and dials it. When the phone rings, she runs to the kitchen and answers it. All very easy for her.

But.

But when Danielle thinks of the future, she thinks of fifth grade, maybe sixth grade. She wishes to be able to graduate from Stoneybrook Elementary. When Kendra thinks of the future, she thinks of college, of being an adult, of becoming a writer. Kendra has a future. Danielle has a future, too, of course, but hers is much more uncertain.

When the last bus had arrived at Baker, one teacher did a head count of the kids who had shown up. Then the others guided their pupils to various areas. One small group went to an art class for extremely disabled kids, another to an art class for more mobile kids, another to physical therapy, etc. Dawn had decided to help in a writing class for fairly mobile students. Kendra was a member of that class.

Into a small room rolled Kendra and six other kids. Four of Kendra's friends rode in motorized wheelchairs. The other two pushed themselves in manual chairs, using strong arms. They positioned themselves in front of computers. Kendra was grinning.

"Today's subject," began Mr Arno, the writing teacher, "is humour. I want you to write a humorous story, and I want you to tell your story in dialogue."

"Just dialogue?" asked a boy.

"Just dialogue," replied Mr Arno.

"Oh, boy!" said Kendra softly. "This is going to be fun."

For the next half hour, Dawn helped the kids with their assignment. Blaire, who's a year older than Kendra, had a lot of questions—and used a voice synthesizer to ask them. Like Kendra, she has cerebral palsy, except that the muscles that control her speech are affected, so she has to communicate by writing or by using her computer. Mickey, who has muscular dystrophy, wrote quickly, his fingers flying over the keys.

"Our champ," said Mr Arno, smiling. "He's taken a typing class."

Mickey had begun to develop muscular dystrophy just a couple of years earlier. So far, his legs were affected, but not his arms.

"However," Mr Arno had told Dawn one

day, "muscular dystrophy is a progressive disease."

"Progressive?" Dawn repeated, watching Mickey.

"Meaning it keeps getting worse."

"Oh." Dawn nodded her head soberly.

That was when I'd realized how silly it was for me to compare children. What was the point of wondering why Danielle had got leukaemia instead of cerebral palsy? Or why Mickey had got muscular dystrophy instead of leukaemia? If he'd got leukaemia, he would still be able to use his legs. But then, he would have been so ill. . . .

Life is not fair, I had reminded myself. Everybody gets a bad break from time to time. The important thing is not what those breaks are, but how you deal with them. If I ever got as ill as Danielle, I hoped I could also be as cheerful and funny and realistic as she was.

I admired Danielle's special brand of hope.

And Dawn admired Kendra's optimism.

"Hey, Dawn," said Kendra, looking up from the computer. "How do you spell 'yo'?"

Dawn laughed. "Y-O," she replied.

"Oh. Just like it sounds. All right." Kendra tapped away at her keyboard. Five minutes later, she said, "Finished!" Then she added, "One day this story is going to be published!"

107

13th
CHAPTER

"The kids are going to be off the wall today," Mr Katz warned me. But he didn't look very concerned. In fact, he was smiling.

Mr Katz and I were getting ready for a Kids Club meeting. I had passed my four-meeting trial and was now the permanent temporary assistant. I would be helping with the club for a few more weeks—until Mrs Simon came back. She had phoned Mr Katz several days earlier to announce her upcoming return. I would be helping for longer than I had originally planned, but Kristy didn't mind.

"Why are the kids going to be off the wall?" I asked.

"The popcorn, for one thing."

The members of the Kids Club had decided to fill goody baskets and deliver them to the elderly people who live at

Stoneybrook Manor. One item in each basket would be a small bag of popcorn. This afternoon was Popcorn Afternoon, when the club members would pop the corn and fill small bags with it.

"Also," continued Mr Katz, "the kids were given vision tests this morning, and this afternoon they had an assembly."

"Oh. They *will* be off the wall, then," I agreed, remembering the excitement over assemblies. And over eye tests, as well.

I was lugging a bag of popcorn kernels onto a desk, when I heard a shriek in the corridor. Then Danielle bounded into the room.

"Danielle? What's going on?" I asked her.

Danielle tried to sober up. "Nothing much," she replied.

"You were shrieking over nothing?"

"Shrieking? Oh, that wasn't me. That was my friend Susanna. I was just telling her the news that Mummy and Daddy told Greg and me at breakfast this morning."

"What news?" I asked.

"Last night Mummy got a phone call. It was from someone at this place called Your Wish Is My Command. They're granting my *wish*. We're going to Disney World! Oh, thank you, Jessi! Mummy told me what you did." Danielle gave me a hug.

"You're going to Disney World?" asked Nicky Pike incredulously.

"Yup," said Danielle. "Mummy and Daddy and Greg and I are going next week for three whole days! We're going to fly to Florida and everything!"

The other kids were arriving.

"Next *week*? During *school*?" squeaked Vanessa.

"Lucky duck," said my sister, smiling. Then she ran across the room and threw her arms around Danielle. "You got your wish!" she exclaimed.

"Yup, I really did."

"What's all this?" Mr Katz asked me.

I explained about YWIMC, and the people I'd talked to there.

"And her wish is being granted?" said Mr Katz. "Fantastic. Jessi, I hope you're feeling particularly proud of yourself right now."

"I—I don't know," I stammered. "I'm just glad the Robertses can go on their holiday. Danielle and Greg will have so much fun."

I looked across the room at Danielle. She was in the centre of a crowd of kids who were leaning over her, peering at something. I wondered what they were looking at. At the same time I noticed something important.

"Mr Katz!" I exclaimed. "Look! The kids are *touching* Danielle. They've forgotten she's ill, I think."

"Finally," murmured Mr Katz, which was the way I felt.

Danielle stood up then, and I saw what she was holding. A book about Disney World. A guide to the Magic Kingdom and EPCOT Center.

"Do you like roller coasters?" Nicky asked Danielle, who nodded. "Then you *have* to go on Space Mountain. It's the best ride."

Danielle was holding a pad of paper. She scribbled something on it.

"*Are* you going during school?" Vanessa asked again.

"Yup."

"Why?"

Danielle shrugged. "Because we just are."

Wendy Jervis, who had been leaning over Danielle's shoulder for a look at the book, suddenly gasped. "Danielle!" she cried.

"What?" Danielle looked alarmed.

"Your—your hair is growing back!" Wendy was staring at the blue plaid scarf covering Danielle's head.

Danielle bit her lip. "I know. It's just started to."

"Mm-hm," said Wendy. "I can see under the scarf in the back. Right here." Wendy pointed to a spot, and the crowd of kids shifted so that they were behind Danielle.

"Hey, your hair's reddish!" exclaimed Peter Tiegreen.

"It wasn't that colour before," added Wendy.

"Well, I told you my hair might change." Danielle looked uncomfortable.

Mr Katz must have noticed, too, because he said, "Okay, kids. Enough."

But Danielle interrupted him. "No," she said. She stood up. Then, slowly, she removed her scarf. Underneath was a stubble of red-brown hair.

What would the kids say?

At first, not much.

Then, they spoke up tentatively.

"I *like* the colour," said Charlotte.

"I wish my hair had red in it," added Wendy.

And Peter, moving around to look at Danielle from the front, said, "Oh, cool! I just realized that you've got the haircut I wanted. Mum wouldn't let me get it, though."

Everyone laughed.

"It really is nice hair," said Vanessa.

"Yeah. Why're you still wearing the scarf?" asked Wendy. "Leave it off."

Mr Katz and I glanced at each other.

"Really?" said Danielle in a small voice.

"Definitely," said Becca. "Hey, can I brush your hair?"

"No, let me." Wendy was waving around a brush. "I have a styling idea."

While Wendy worked on Danielle's hair, the other kids continued to bombard her with questions about Disney World.

"Would you get me a pair of mouse ears—if I give you the money?"

"Are you going to stay in a hotel with a pool?"

"Do you think your parents will let you ride Space Mountain twice?"

"Are you going to go to the park with the water rides?"

Danielle attempted to answer the questions. Finally, she said, "I've never *been* to Disney World! I can't tell you that much. How about if I write you all a postcard while I'm in Florida?"

"And take lots of pictures," suggested Peter.

"Yeah, get someone to take a picture of you and Goofy," said Nicky.

At that point Mr Katz wandered over to the members of the Kids Club and said, "Maybe the hair salon ought to close down for a while. We have goody baskets to put together. The popcorn is waiting to be popped."

"Right," said Danielle agreeably. "Can I just see how I look first?"

Seven kids dived for mirrors and handed them to Danielle.

She chose one, held it before her face, and admired herself. "Thanks, Wendy," she said after a moment. "I like that hairstyle. I don't look the way I used to, but—"

"You look really nice," Peter supplied. "You look cool."

"Ready, kids?" said Mr Katz.

"Ready!" they chorused.

"All right. We have three poppers. Please divide yourself into three groups."

The kids did so quickly. Then Mr Katz explained how the poppers operated, and he and I hovered around the kids as they got to work.

"What else are we going to put in the goody baskets?" asked Mr Katz, as the kids made batches of popcorn and filled small bags, tying each one with a red ribbon. They worked industriously, concentrating on making perfect popcorn (no burned kernels) and perfect bows on the bags.

"What do old people like?" asked Wendy.

"Wendy!" cried Danielle. "Old people are just the same as any other people. They like all sorts of things."

"But some of them don't have many teeth," Wendy objected.

"And some of them have all their teeth," replied Danielle. "Come on. Let's think about what we'd want if we were stuck in . . . oh, a hospital."

"What did *you* want when you were in the hospital?" asked Charlotte.

"I wanted to go home." Danielle giggled.

"What did you want to *eat*?" pressed Charlotte.

"Mmm. Treats. Popcorn is a good choice. Maybe some chocolate peppermints."

"Grown-ups like disgusting stuff, like caviar," announced Nicky.

"Do the goody baskets have to be full of food?" asked Danielle. "I got bored in the hospital. Maybe the people at Stoneybrook Manor would want things to keep them busy. We could put crossword puzzles in the baskets."

"Paperback books," added my sister.

"Pens for writing letters, or maybe poems," suggested Vanessa.

"How about photos of us?" said Bruce, who liked using the Polaroid.

"Yeah, photos!" exclaimed Danielle.

Half the kids had abandoned the poppers. Once again they were crowded around Danielle, talking eagerly.

"Are you kids paying attention to the—" Mr Katz began to say.

BANG! The lid exploded off one of the poppers. It sailed across the room and crashed into a bookshelf. From the popper erupted a shower of popcorn.

"Poppers?" Mr Katz finished.

"No?" suggested Danielle.

Mr Katz smiled. So did I. The kids began

to laugh. Then Danielle and her friends
flopped onto the floor and began to clear up
the popcorn.

14th CHAPTER

"Please, please, please? Can we leave, leave, leave?" sang Becca.

"Too bad 'please' and 'leave' don't rhyme," said Charlotte.

"Oh, it doesn't matter." Becca was hopping around our kitchen. "If you must know, it's time to go!" she continued.

"Becca, can you come here for a sec?" I asked. I pulled my sister into the living room. "You are annoying Aunt Cecelia," I hissed.

"But I'm ready to go to Danielle's."

"I know. So am I. So is Charlotte. But Squirt isn't. Just let Aunt Cecelia finish dressing him, okay? He got all sticky."

My sister was unbelievably excited. She had run through the door from school about twenty minutes earlier. Now she was ready to spend the afternoon at the Robertses' house. Early the next morning, Danielle and her family would leave for Florida. Becca and Charlotte and I had been invited over to help Danielle pack and get ready for the trip.

And to say goodbye.

"Just calm down long enough to let Aunt Cecelia put Squirt's dungarees on him," I whispered to Becca. "Then we can go."

Fifteen minutes later, Aunt Cecelia pulled up in front of Danielle's house. Becca and Charlotte exploded out of the car. I followed more slowly. "Thanks, Aunt Cecelia," I called. "Daddy said he'd pick us up at six o'clock."

Aunt Cecelia and Squirt drove off and I ran to the Robertses' front step. Danielle was letting Charlotte and Becca inside.

"Hi, Jessi!" she yelled.

"Hi!" I replied.

"Come and help me pack!"

Danielle ran to her bedroom, Becca, Charlotte, and I ran after her.

"Danielle! Slow down!" called Mrs Roberts.

"She has been saying that all afternoon," said Danielle. But she did slow down.

"Excited?" I asked as I entered Danielle's room.

It was an unnecessary question. The room itself told me the answer. It was the biggest mess I had ever seen. Mama would have described it simply as a "sight". Clothes were *every*where—on the floor, strewn across the bed, under chairs. A shirt was draped over a lampshade. Two suitcases yawned open. Both were already full—mostly of toys and books.

"Why are you packing your toys?" asked Becca.

She said that at the same time that I pointed to the lampshade and said, "What's happened to your shirt?"

Danielle looked at the shirt and frowned. "I don't know *how* it got there," she said, mystified.

"Hey! I can smell something burning!" exclaimed Charlotte.

Smoke rose from the lamp. I grabbed the shirt off it. A hole was smouldering in the back.

"Uh-oh," said Danielle. "I'd better calm down."

"You'd better clean up this pigsty," said her mother from the hallway.

Danielle settled down—sort of. She removed the toys from her suitcases. "I suppose I don't *really* need these," she remarked.

"Yeah, who needs toys at Disney World?" said Charlotte.

"I'll just pack all these clothes," Danielle went on.

Mrs Roberts was listening from her bedroom. "We're only going to be away for three days," she reminded Danielle. "Pack *one* suitcase, please."

Giggling, Danielle jammed the clothes into the larger suitcase.

"Did you remember some sunscreen?" asked Charlotte. "Florida will be hot."

"Did you pack your bathing suit?" asked Becca.

"Sunglasses?" I added.

"Yipes," said Danielle. "Maybe I'd better start again. How many dresses should I take? Four?"

"None!" cried Becca, Charlotte and I.

Danielle emptied out the suitcase, put away the dresses, and started again. When she'd finally finished, the four of us collapsed on the floor.

"These are going to be the best three days," said Danielle. She sighed. "*Every*thing will be great. The aeroplane ride. Oh, we get to eat breakfast on the plane. I've never eaten scrambled eggs in the sky."

"Maybe you'll have something more delicious than eggs. Maybe you'll eat French toast in the sky," said Charlotte dreamily.

"Yeah," said Danielle. "And when the plane lands, we'll be in Florida. Nice warm weather, palm trees. And we'll stay in a hotel."

"After you see the hotel, you'll go to . . . Disney World," I added.

"Micky, Minnie, Donald, Goofy, Tigger," chanted my sister.

"You know what, Jessi?" said Danielle. "I wish you could come with us."

"Me, too," I replied. "But you and your mum and dad and Greg are going to have a great time. Just your family. All together."

At six o'clock, Daddy arrived. He honked the horn from the street.

"We have to go, Danielle," said Becca.

"I'll write lots of postcards," Danielle promised. "I'll write to all of you. And to Mr Katz. And to the Kids Club. Goodbye, you lot!"

Charlotte and Becca and I ran to the car.

Danielle kept her promise. She did write lots of postcards. They arrived after the Robertses came home, but that was okay.

Dear Jessi,
   We are on the plane. It has not even taken off yet! But it will soon. There's a pocket on the back of the seat in front of me. Here's what is inside. A magazine. An old newspaper. A sick BAG!
                              Love,
                                 Danielle

Dear Charlotte,
  We are in the sky. We are flying.
I wish I could really fly.
That reminds me. I want to
go on the Peter Pan ride at
WDW (Walt Disney World).
We just got breakfast. Guess
what! We are eating pan-
cakes and ~~sausig~~ ~~sauseer~~
sausages in the sky!
                    Love,
                    Danielle

Dear Becca,
  The plane is landing. Greg had
to use his sick bag. He is so
gross. I am not going to ride on
Space Mountain with him. He
can be sick on someone else. Uh-oh.
We just landed. We're in Florida!
This afternoon we will be at
WDW. I cannot ~~weight~~ wait!
I cannot wait!
                    Love, Danielle

Dear Mr. Katz,

   I am writing to you from our hotel room. This postcard was free. I found it in the drawer of the dresser. There is some ~~stash~~ ~~staf~~ writing paper and envelopes and pens, too. Daddy said I could keep the pen. In one half of an hour we are going to WDW.

                  Sincerely, Danielle

Dear Jessi,

   We spent the hole afternoon at WDW. I rode Space Mountain two times. Did you know that the people at YWMC were going to fix things so that me and my family get to go to the head of every line? No waiting! Mummy says at this rate we will get to go on every ride twice. She looks tired.

                  Love ya, Danielle

Dear Kids Club,
   Here I am in Disney World.
I mean, I really am in
Disney World. My father and
me are sitting at a table in
Fantasyland. Mummy and
Greg are in Tomorrowland. (I
just need a little rest. Daddy
and I are eating ice cream.)
Last night we saw fireworks.
Today we'll see a parade.
              Miss ya! Danielle

DEAR BECCA!!!!!
   I HAD MY PICTURE TAKEN
WITH MICKEY MOUSE !!!!!!!
            LUV, DANIELLE!!!!!

Dear Charlotte,
   We spent today at EPCOT Center.
Greg loved the dinosaur ride.
I liked it too but I liked
shopping at all the different
lands even better.
            Love, Danielle

Dear Jessi,
   We have to come home this
evening. ☹ I had so much
fun here. I wish I could live at
Disney World. I would be sure
to ride Space Mountain once a
day. I would have ice cream
for breakfast. Mummy said
maybe we can see the parade
one more time. See you soon!
                 Love, Danielle

The Robertses flew home on Thursday
night. They got in late, so Danielle and
Greg were allowed to stay at home on
Friday. But they were back at school on
Monday, and on Tuesday, I saw Danielle at
the Kids Club meeting. Her return was
triumphant. She turned up with presents
for everyone. Each member of the Kids
Club, except Becca and Charlotte, got a
Mickey Mouse sticker. Danielle had chosen
special presents for Becca, Charlotte,
Mr Katz, and me. For Becca, a Donald
Duck T-shirt. For Charlotte, a book about
Disney World. For Mr Katz, mouse ears
with "Mr K." written on the back. And for
me, a delicate silver necklace in the shape of
a star.

"It's a wishing star," Danielle told me. "Because you helped make one of my wishes come true. I'll never forget that."

"Thank you," I said seriously.

Danielle grinned. "Thank *you*. You know what? The trip to Disney World was the best trip ever. It made my life!"

15th
CHAPTER

It was my last day with the Kids Club. The following week, Miss Simon would be back. Actually, she had already returned to Stoneybrook, but she was taking her time getting involved with school and the club again.

I had planned a surprise for the kids. I was going to show them how to make Christmas wreaths from coat hangers and tissue paper. Then, in December, they could make wreaths to decorate Stoneybrook Manor, the hospital, and any other place they could think of.

Mr Katz and I got out a stack of metal coat hangers, a pile of green tissue paper, and a smaller pile of red construction paper (for holly berries). We put the things on a table at the front of the room.

"Will you be glad to get back to babysitting?" Mr Katz asked me.

I nodded. "Yes. But I'll miss the Kids Club."

"Well, glad as we are to have Miss Simon back, we'll miss you, too, Jessi. The kids adored having you. And of course they're delighted that there still *is* a Kids Club."

"Thanks. I adored being here. And *I'm* glad there's still a Kids Club, too. For Becca's sake. For Danielle's. . . . For a lot of reasons."

"Hey, I'm he-ere!" shouted Peter Tiegreen. He ran into the room, bouncing an imaginary basketball. "He shoots!" he said under his breath, "and . . . *yes*! He makes it! Two points. The crowd goes wild."

Nicky Pike arrived next. His shoes were untied, and he tripped over the laces, fell, and stood up as if nothing had happened.

"It is the *best* book," I heard Becca say, as she and Charlotte came into the room. "You *have* to read it. I'm telling you if you don't, you're missing something good. It's called *Number the Stars*. Remember that."

A few minutes later, Mr Katz raised his voice. "Are you ready to begin, kids? Is everyone here?"

I was searching the room. "Danielle isn't," I pointed out.

"Was Danielle at school today?" asked Mr Katz.

The kids became unnaturally quiet.

"No," answered Peter.

Wendy raised her hand hesitantly. "Um, I heard she's in hospital again," she said, almost in a whisper.

I felt as if the floor gave way beneath me. I actually had to steady myself by reaching for the back of a chair.

Mr Katz looked at the solemn faces. "Is that just a rumour?" he asked.

"I suppose so," replied Wendy. "But I heard it from my teacher. And she heard it from Greg Roberts."

Oh, no. Oh, *no*. This wasn't fair. What had happened?

"What happened?" I asked Wendy.

"I'm not sure," she replied. "My teacher didn't say."

I looked across the room at Becca. She was crying silently. Tears ran down her cheeks and dripped onto her shirt. Next to her, Charlotte was also crying.

I pulled myself together. "Mr Katz," I whispered. "I'm going to take Becca and Charlotte outside for a few minutes. I'll bring them right back."

Mr Katz glanced at the girls, then nodded.

I led Becca and Charlotte into the corridor. Behind me, I could hear Mr Katz saying, "What would you rather do first today? Start making Christmas wreaths, or write letters to Danielle?"

I couldn't hear the kids' answer, but that

didn't matter. I didn't need to. I knew what they would decide.

"Come on, you two. Let's go to the girls' toilets," I said.

"Okay," Becca replied, sniffing.

We walked down the corridor and I pushed open the door to the cloakroom. The girls followed me inside.

"Sit on a windowsill," I instructed them.

"We're not allowed to," replied Charlotte.

"Just this once," I said. "If you get caught, I'll take the blame."

The girls climbed slowly onto the sill and sat there, looking at me, tears still running down their cheeks. My chest ached. That was how hard I was trying not to cry with them.

Before I could say a word, Becca said just what I'd been thinking: "It isn't fair. It isn't fair at all. Danielle is too nice."

I held onto Becca's hands. "No. It isn't fair," I agreed. "But it happened. Just like a lot of unfair things that happen. It isn't fair that Stacey has diabetes. It isn't fair that people sometimes tease you because your skin is darker than theirs. It isn't fair that parents get divorced. War isn't fair. But those things happen, and then we have to deal with them."

Charlotte looked thoughtful. "You know what?" she said. "We don't even know why

Danielle is in hospital. We just decided she was ill again. But maybe she fell down and broke her leg or something."

"Maybe," said Becca, "but I don't really think so. Do you?"

"No," replied Charlotte in a small voice. She began to sob. "I don't . . . I don't" (she could hardly speak) "I don't want Danielle to be ill."

"I don't want her to die," added Becca.

"Neither do I," I said. "Let's concentrate on Danielle's doctors. Let's hope they're taking extra good care of her. She does have a chance of beating the leukaemia, you know. Maybe we can help her along."

"We'll still be her friends," said Charlotte.

"Of course," I agreed.

"Remember Danielle said she would get bored in the hospital? We should write letters to her. And send her stuff," Charlotte went on.

"Good idea," I said. "She'll be glad to know you're thinking of her." I paused. "You know what?" I went on. "If you go back to the Kids Club now, you can write letters to Danielle this very second. I think that's what the others are doing. Are you ready to go back?"

"I suppose so," said Becca.

"Me, too," said Charlotte. "Do we look as if we've been crying?"

"A little," I answered. "Why don't you wash your faces first?"

The girls washed their faces and returned to Mr Katz's room.

That night I talked to my mother. "Mama?" I said. Dinner was over. I was trying to do my homework, but I couldn't keep my mind on it. Mama had come into my room and was sitting on the end of the bed.

"You're thinking about Danielle, aren't you?"

I nodded. "I really want to know what's going on. I *need* to know. So do Becca and Charlotte. Do you think it would be okay to phone Danielle at the hospital? I'd only talk to her for a few minutes."

"I know, you would, darling," said Mama. "But I think maybe you *shouldn't* phone. Not yet. How about writing her a letter? Did you write one this afternoon with the kids?"

"No. I just helped the kids. With spelling and stuff."

"Then why don't *you* write? You're pretty special to Danielle. I'm sure she'd want to hear from you. I also think she'd want to answer you. Let you know what's going on."

I nodded. "Thanks, Mama," I said. "I'll write to her this very minute. Then I'll do my homework. I promise I can finish it."

132

"Okay." Mama smoothed back my hair. She stood up to leave.

"Hey!" I exclaimed. "I've just had an idea. Could I phone the Robertses' at home?"

Mama looked thoughtful. "I don't see why not," she said after a moment.

I ran to my parents' room and dialled Danielle's number.

Greg answered the phone.

"Hi!" I cried. "It's Jessi!" Greg didn't say anything, so I continued, "Um, I heard Danielle is—is back in hospital."

"Yeah."

"Well . . . what happened?"

"She wasn't feeling well. The doctors wanted to do some tests."

"She's in just for tests?" I repeated. That didn't sound so bad.

"Yeah," said Greg again.

He didn't want to talk, that was clear. So I ended the conversation. I was feeling better, though. I returned to my room and wrote a cheerful note to Danielle. I ended by saying:

Everybody misses you. Especially me. And Becca and Charlotte. And Mr Katz. And Wendy. Like

I said, everyone misses you! And we're thinking about you. We hope you come home soon. Becca wants to play with Mr Toes again. And with you, too, of course.

I hope you aren't too bored in the hospital. If you are, try to unbore yourself. Do you want some crossword puzzle books?

Miss ya!

Jessi

Four days later I came home from school and found a letter addressed to me lying on the kitchen table. The handwriting looked familiar, but I couldn't quite place it. I turned over the envelope. It was from Danielle! (She was still in hospital.)

I tore open the envelope, and read the letter quickly:

Dear Jessi,

Hi! I got your letter. Thanks! It came right when I was really bored, but it unbored me right away. I got letters from everyone in the Kids Club, too. I am trying to answer them all. That keeps me pretty busy. Plus mommy makes me do my homework and stuff.

I have bad news and good news. The bad news is that the doctors aren't sure when I can come home. Maybe not for a little while. The good news is that I am very hopeful. About everything. After all, I used to have two wishes, and one of them has already come true. So maybe the other will, too. Mommy and Daddy say, "Think positively," so I do.

See you soon!
'Bye

Love
Danielle

Sorry
Sloppy

I folded Danielle's letter and replaced it in the envelope.

Wishes *do* come true, I told myself. So I wished my wish again.

Please get better, Danielle.

THE BABYSITTERS CLUB MYSTERIES

Our favourite Babysitters are super-sleuths too! Don't miss the new series of Babysitters Club Mysteries:

No 1: Stacey and the Missing Ring
When Stacey's accused of stealing a valuable ring from a new family she's been sitting for, she's devastated – Stacey is *not* a thief! One way or another the Babysitters have *got* to find that ring and save the reputation of the Club . . . before it's too late!

No 2: Beware! Dawn
Just *who* is the mysterious "Mr X" who's been sending threatening notes to Dawn and phoning her while she's babysitting, *alone*? Dawn is determined to get to the bottom of this mystery, but she's *pretty* scared . . . what if she's in real danger?

Look out for:

No 3: Mallory and the Ghost Cat
No 4: Kristy and the Missing Child
No 5: Mary Anne and the Secret in the Attic
No 6: The Mystery at Claudia's House